SPACE COCAINE

SPACE COCAINE

contents

Rogue   **1**
.... Jessie Kwak

Namasté Prime   **19**
.... Grá Linnaea

My Work Will Change the World   **51**
.... A. W. McCollough

The Cosmic Game
    I: The Vacation Not Taken   **89**
.... Mark Teppo

Rogue

Jessie Kwak

Normally when a job starts to go this bad, it's a logistics issue. Somebody didn't think through all the options, one thread snags, and then the whole plan unravels into a mess.

That's something Willem Jaantzen can deal with.

But this time? Someone on *this* job is deliberately snagging threads.

If Jaantzen's learned anything in his first, rough, twenty-four years of life, it's that survival is all about watching your own back and having an exit plan to get out with your fair share when things go sideways. Problem is, Jaantzen normally takes jobs down on solid ground where he can melt back into the city. He's not used to this space pirate shit. Being trapped in a tin can hurtling through the skies above New Sarjun with another—smaller—tin can as his only way home is not his idea of a good time.

But a job's a job.

And damned if he's going to die in space.

Dez is pretty fast with his knife, but Jaantzen is even faster with a gun—even with this lightweight electric piece Amita insisted he carry instead of his usual pistol with the hull-tearing large-cal bullets. His first electric bolt hits Dez square in the temple, and though it may not pack a big punch—Jaantzen has been shot with one plenty of times before—it'll fry someone's wires if you hit them where it counts.

Dez's been hit where it counts.

The other man goes still, but he doesn't fall, just floats in the zero G of the luxury yacht's cargo hold, all loose joints and slack jaw, a patch of flesh on his pale temple singed bubblegum pink and carbon black and stinking with smoke.

"Not today, asshole," Jaantzen mutters, shoving the electric pistol back into its holster and giving Dez a gentle push to float him out of the way.

Jaantzen shoulders Dez's bag as well, then pushes the heavy rubber crate awkwardly out of the cargo hold and into the corridor. One silver lining of the head-spinning weightlessness on this docked yacht? Down on New Sarjun he'd be screwed getting the goods back home after shooting his partner.

Still, the rubber crate is ungainly, bumping off Jaantzen's shins and scuffing the immaculate cream lacquer of the walls. Even in the lower deck, the hallway's handholds are gold plated. Pry one of these off and Jaantzen will eat well for a month. Pry all of them off and he won't have to work for Amita any more. He could start his own outfit, maybe. Choose his own jobs.

Think of the Devil, and Amita's voice crackles in his ear.

"Dez, Jaantzen. What happened?"

"Dez tried to doublecross us," Jaantzen answers. "I've got the goods."

A pause. He pictures the face Amita's probably making at this very moment: one eye narrowing, lips quirked to the side as she decides who's bullshitting her. She made that same face ten years ago when she found Willem Jaantzen fresh from breaking out of the orphanage, lost in the wrong gang's territory. He'd been just some soft kid trying to convince her he'd be worth keeping alive, that he'd work out to be more than just another mouth to feed.

Amita's pause is brief; she didn't fight her way to the top of her crew by making slow decisions.

"Copy that," she says. "Let's get out of here."

Jaantzen awkwardly ricochets into a ladderway and propels the crate up toward the docking bay.

Time to get off this boat.

And to find out who else on the crew Dez was working with.

It would be a simple job, Amita had said. A luxury yacht, the *Dahlia Regina* with a cargo hold full of drugs—raw Indiran snow. Real, not synth, she'd said with a gleam in her eye that said she'd tried both and knew the difference.

Jaantzen just understood it would fetch a better price. Even if he could afford it, he wasn't interested in the baggage that came with tasting that honey.

The yacht's owner would be down on New Sarjun brokering a deal with one of the nightclub owners in Bulari's Tamarind District, Amita had said. No real security on the boat, on account of nobody would be stupid enough to try to hit it while it was in orbit.

Amita'd smiled as she'd said this last. She's not stupid, but he suspects she thinks he is. Her own hunk of muscle with no ambition of his own, at her beck and call whenever she needs somebody with a gun for one of her many jobs.

Jaantzen's not stupid, either. But he's broke, and he's worked with Amita on enough jobs to know she doesn't go in without an exit plan. The trick to working for her is making sure you're part of that plan.

"Just me and you?" he'd asked.

She'd shaken her head. "I've got a pilot, a tech, another gun, you, and me."

"Five?" Jaantzen hadn't liked five. Hell, Jaantzen doesn't like jobs that require more than two, tops, but the paydays are only so big when you're working on your own. Sometimes you gotta trust somebody else not to shoot you—at least not until closer to the end of the job.

Amita'd given him that half smile, golden-brown eyes locked on his, the look that says, *I know you're going to do it, I'm just waiting for you to say yes.*

And Jaantzen had just shrugged. What the hell. He'd never been in space.

Might as well see if it's everything it's cracked up to be.

★

Turns out jobs with Amita in space are just as messy as jobs with Amita on solid ground, only with a side of terrible, gut-curdling weightlessness.

Jaantzen pushes the crate up the last ladderway and bites out a curse.

Dez was the other gun, and Beetle is the tech, all wiry and lean, tawny brown skin and a shock-purple hair done up in a mass of skinny braids.

Currently, Beetle is dead at the console in the bridge, quivering droplets of blood pearling away from a knife stuck in his spinal column. Since he was supposed to hack the security settings that would get them off this boat, this is not a good sign.

It wasn't Dez, since Dez never left Jaantzen's side. His gut says Haruko, the pilot, but Jaantzen isn't trusting enough to rule out Amita. Could be she brought along a crew she thinks is disposable.

Willem Jaantzen is not disposable.

"Amita, come in," he says.

Jaantzen activates his grav boots beside the console, stumbling briefly as the magnets catch. Beetle's floating face-down over the control panel; Jaantzen shifts him gently out of the way. The tech's hand trails behind him as he floats out of the chair, leaving a smear of sticky blood on the console's glass.

Computers aren't Jaantzen's thing, but the green outlines around the docking clamps that have hold of their shuttle looks like all systems go. Hopefully Beetle got through the security before getting knifed—but that's no longer their biggest problem.

A proximity alert is blinking in the corner of the screen. Jaantzen swipes it open and growls with frustration. It's an Alliance cutter, making a beeline directly toward them.

Amita still hasn't answered. Jaantzen's got the goods, so there's no way she took off without getting a payday. Why isn't she responding?

"Amita."

But there's something off in the silence around his voice. The connection's been cut.

Jaantzen whirls just as a pop from a handheld electric barb sounds. The barbs zip past him and clink off the console, wires flailing.

He blocks the electric barb with enough force that it goes flying from his attacker's hand, then punches them in the jaw before they can react. Jaantzen's ready to grapple, but he's unprepared for the *Dahlia Regina*, where his gravboots suck at his feet like mud and his assailant—a woman with a thick braid of blond hair—goes flying out of reach from the force of his punch, crashing against the navigation array.

She's not alone. Her companion takes aim.

For such a big ship, the yacht's bridge is cramped: the nav console takes up a third of the space with its chrome plated panels, and a pair of chairs—one of which is taken up by Beetle's body—are bolted to the floor. It's not nearly enough space for the three-person shootout Jaantzen's attackers seem to be planning, but it's perfect for a brawl.

Jaantzen can brawl.

He launches himself at the second assailant—a tawny man with long, wavy black hair—and catches him around the midriff before he can fire. They crash into a wall panel; there's a shriek of metal hinges as the panel's thin metal door crumples under the impact.

The man's tall and lithe, but what he knows about fighting in zero G isn't a match for Jaantzen's bulk and strength. With his opponent securely pinned against the wall, Jaantzen clocks him in the jaw—once, twice—and then his own head rings with a blow from behind.

The woman's caught him with a flying kick, ricocheting gracefully to catch herself on the ladder and crouch like a cat ready to spring.

When she does, Jaantzen locks his gravboots and twists, using her companion's back as a shield to deflect her. But he's not expecting the man's effortless weight. He almost loses control, then the man is grinning as he corkscrews deftly in Jaantzen's hands, breaking free. His knee catches Jaantzen under the chin as he spins away.

Toward the electric barb, which is floating near the ceiling.

Jaantzen launches himself after it, and what he lacks in zero G grace, he makes up for in size, catching the man once more and locking his gravboots to the ceiling, using his mass to pin the man in place beneath him.

He pulls his electric pistol, and lodges it between the man's eyes.

The man moves slowly, lifting hands above head and slowly releasing the electric barb he's just caught, sending the weapon floating out of reach. A smile spreads across his face, rakish through bloodied lips. "Not a bad fight for a grounder," he says. His accent, that brash lilt: he's from Durga's Belt. "But it looks like we're at an impasse."

His black eyes twinkle, then roll meaningfully to Jaantzen's right.

Jaantzen spares a glance to see the woman aiming her own gun squarely at his own head; a faint, familiar whine fills the room as the weapon warms to her palm. It's not an electric stun pistol like what Jaantzen has. Jaantzen's will do serious damage to the man at this range, but hers will tear through the hull if she doesn't aim true.

That calm look in her eyes says she tends to aim true.

For a moment, Jaantzen fights pure vertigo as he realizes they're on the ceiling, the woman standing on the floor with Beetle's body drifting beside her. He focuses his attention back on his captive before he loses it.

"Did you kill my tech guy?" Jaantzen says.

"No," the man says. "It was a tall guy, pale. Black buzz cut?"

Haruko, the pilot. Jaantzen feels a thrill of fear for Amita, chased by the realization that Haruko could possibly be working on her orders and she's planning on double crossing Jaantzen, instead.

Whatever the man sees on Jaantzen's face causes him to smile sadly. "Another one of yours, then? The crew you run with is a mess."

Jaantzen's not in a place to pick who he works with, and he's not about to have a heart-to-heart with this asteroid-belt pirate. He needs to get rid of these two, schlep the cargo back to the docking bay without Dez or Beetle to help, and either sweet talk Amita into not ditching him in space or help her fight Haruko, depending on the situation.

And he needs to do it fast.

Because that Alliance ship he noticed earlier? It's hailing them.

"*Dahlia Regina*, this is the Alliance patrol vessel *Andaluz*. We're receiving a distress signal, and will board if we receive no reply."

"This was excellent choice of target, if I do say so myself," the man says. "If unfortunately executed on all our sides. But I think we can still salvage the day. Pirate's honor, spoils go to the victor. Particularly when it's the victor's home turf."

Jaantzen frowns at him. "What do you mean?"

"We raided a resupply ship heading to the Arquellian embassy on New Sarjun just a few days ago, and we picked up quite the feast in Arquellian delicacies. We'd be happy to give you dinner and a ride back home on the *Nanshe*."

At the name, Jaantzen's eyes widen. He may not pay much attention to what happens off New Sarjun, but the exploits of the captain of the *Nanshe* get around.

"You're Raj Dusai."

"At your service." Raj gives him another bright smile. A thread of blood drifts from his nose. "Allow me to introduce my wife, Lasadi."

Lasadi tips her chin in greeting, but her aim doesn't waver.

"You give me a ride planetside? And what do I give you."

"For starters, you take that gun away from my head, and we get a move on so we can get off the ship before the

Alliance catch us. We stand here—excuse me, lay here—bartering much longer, we're all rotting away in prison."

Jaantzen doesn't move.

"You can trust us," Raj says. "Of course everyone says that. But if you know who I am, you know the Dusais keep their word."

"Nobody keeps their word."

Behind him—below him—Lasadi laughs. "Maybe you've just been running with the wrong crew."

"*Dahlia Regina*, this is the Alliance patrol vessel *Andaluz*. We're now attempting to board. Be aware that we will treat anyone on board as hostile."

"I let go of my weapon and your wife shoots me," Jaantzen says.

"Where's the honor in that?" Lasadi says. "But I guarantee if you harm Raj, your brains will be a fresh coat of paint on this gaudy-ass ship."

"It could use some redecorating," Jaantzen says, but he finally sits back, and slips his electric pistol back into its holster at the small of his back. He risks another look at Lasadi Dusai, and his stomach clenches once more with vertigo at clinging to the ceiling while she stands on the floor.

Lasadi holsters her own weapon, and Jaantzen releases his gravboots, pushing off Raj's body gently in an attempt to get his feet right on the true floor. He's overspinning, but Lasadi rights him effortlessly despite being half his size. Raj pushes from the ceiling gracefully as a cat.

Jaantzen lets out a string of curses.

The cargo—the payday—is gone.

"Amita!" he yells, knowing for sure the line of communication is cut. It's a yell of frustration and rage, equal parts fear for her safety and fury at the possibility she's betrayed him.

In response he hears a blood-curdling scream of pain. The voice is distorted and raw, but Jaantzen would recognize it anywhere. It's torn from the throat of the person he's known longer than anyone in his life: Amita. He pushes himself up the stairwell toward the docking bay at the rear of the *Dahlia Regina*, forgetting the notorious space pirates behind him.

"Kid, wait!" he hears Raj shout.

Amita's floating in the docking bay when they arrive, limbs sprawled like somebody's forgotten doll, the ozone scorch of an electric pistol still lingering in the air. Her eyes are blinking rapidly—Jaantzen knows that look of someone who's been stunned, her nervous system overloaded and shut down. But she's still alive.

Haruko is loading the cargo onto their shuttle, a piece of trash that barely looks spaceworthy on its own, let alone in comparison to the gleaming yacht whose docking bay it currently fills.

The blast from Haruko's electric pistol just grazes Jaantzen's arm. He feels the flash of heat, the sharp bite of electricity in his bicep spidering out through his body. His hair stands on end, his fingertips tingle. If the shot had hit him square on, his arm would be useless.

Jaantzen fires back, but zero G is shit for proper footing and the shot goes wide to hit the doorway to the shuttle.

The doorway arcs a moment with flickering blue. Jaantzen curses himself: one wrong hit and the shuttle's dead.

"C'mon, kid," Raj says beside him. "It's not worth it."

The shuttle door is closing, Haruko mashing at the controls beside it. If Jaantzen launches himself now, he might just make it through, might just be able to catch Haruko and, what? Put a gun to his head and forced him to fly them both home? Leaving Amita floating there for the Alliance to find? She'll likely turn on him someday, but apparently today was not that day. He'll defend himself when that day comes, but he won't be the first to turn.

"I bought us a few more minutes," Lasadi calls. She's been furiously typing commands into the control panel by the bay airlock.

"*Dahlia Regina*, this is the Alliance patrol *Andaluz*. Release control of the docking doors immediately, or we will respond with lethal force."

The shuttle's engines rev.

"He's getting control of airlock," Lasadi yells. "If we don't get out of here immediately we're spaced." She pushes herself away from the control panel, rocketing toward the far end of the docking bay, where a panel in the wall has been pushed aside. "Raj, now!"

"You coming or you dying, kid?" Raj Dusai asks Jaantzen.

"Not without my crew." Jaantzen pushes himself over to Amita, catches her in midair; she's struggling to swallow, eyes wild and limbs stiff. She's impossibly light.

"Let's go then."

A warning begins to sound as the depressurization sequence begins. Jaantzen isn't sure where Raj and Lasadi are parked, but he knows that the Alliance like to have a scapegoat—especially when they've been pissed off. He fires his electric pistol at the shuttle's docking clamps, then again at the engines. A net of blue electricity crackles over the shuttle, and the docking mechanism convulses once then sticks open, clinging to the floor of the docking bay. The engine whines and begins to smoke.

Through the glass panel, Haruko is screaming something Jaantzen can't hear. Jaantzen lets him scream, grabs Amita by the shoulders and maneuvers her over to the far end of the docking bay where Raj Dusai is waiting to help pull her through the passageway.

It's a short glide to the hole Raj and Lasadi have lased in the hull of the luxury yacht. Lasadi's there already, smearing the edges of the cutout section with a golden goo.

"Try not to touch this, big guy," she says as Jaantzen passes Amita through to her. Jaantzen doesn't have Amita's slight build, nor Rajs, nor Lasadi's. But he manages to get his wide shoulders through without disturbing the goo—mostly. He helps Lasadi maneuver the plate back into place, and the two edges fuse together with the fizzle. Through the airlock, and Lasadi points him to the cramped cockpit where Raj has already strapped Amita into a seat.

Nobody says anything as they release the airlock and Raj shoves off from the *Dahlia Regina*. The outline of the yacht fills the viewscreen, all gold-and-green paint and stylish lines. They float a moment nose-to-nose with the yacht while Jaantzen's fingers curl around his armrests. They should be flying out of here as fast as possible, not sticking around. What are they doing?

Hiding from the Alliance cutter, he realizes. The docking bay doors are on the far side of the yacht, and the Alliance won't have visual on them while they're docking. Nor will their proximity sensors be triggered while the *Nanshe* is merely drifting.

"They're in," Lasadi says. She taps a sequence into the console in front of her. "I overrode the *Dahlia*'s quick release; they're not going anywhere for a bit.

"Love it," says Raj. "Strap in, kid."

Raj pivots the *Nanshe* and hits the thrusters, the force of the movement pressing Jaantzen into the seat as gravity suddenly shifts in yet another flush of vertigo. And either the Alliance cutter doesn't see them, can't undock in time, or ignores them in favor of Haruko trapped in his shuttle with crates of raw Indiran snow.

Whatever the reason, they're home free.

After a time, the pressure lets up, and Jaantzen is weightless once more. Raj is humming absently into the silence; Amita's breath comes ragged and slow.

Your crew's a mess, Raj had said. And, yeah. Sure. It is. But where the hell are you supposed to find people to trust? He's known Amita almost half of his life, but he's still not sure she won't sell him out the minute things go south.

"I guess you didn't get your payday," Jaantzen says. Neither did they, but at least he and Amita got out of here alive. He can only hope Amita was pulling this job on spec, rather than with the backing of a potential buyer.

Jaantzen can see only the curve of Lasadi's cheek lit by the instrument panel, but there's no missing that slow smile. "We got what we came here for," she says. "The cargo would have fetched a good price, but secrets? That's where the real money's at." She turns and her gaze slides past him to Amita; the smile fades. "Check on your friend."

Jaantzen disentangles himself from his harness and lets himself float over to Amita. She has a burn sear on her right collarbone, the wound blistered and weeping. But her breathing is more or less normal, now. She blinks, focuses on Jaantzen.

"You almost got yourself killed for me," she whispers, voice coming harsh through raw vocal chords. "Why?"

"It's what crew does," Jaantzen says. What crew *should* do, anyhow.

Amita's gaze cuts down, hands tight on the armrests. Jaantzen doesn't like the half-guilty way she's trying not to look at him, so he turns away to see Raj and Lasadi leaning together over the controls. Not just crew, but partners. Lovers. Family. They're not talking as they navigate together. Like their fighting style, they're perfectly paired without having to discuss it.

Lasadi leans companionably over Raj to flick a switch on his console, and Raj's body responds almost unconsciously to accommodate her, a small smile on his lips as she brushes a hand over her thigh.

Jaantzen clears his throat.

"You're going to drop us off?"

"It's not safe for us to hit surface at the moment," Raj says, "not with the Alliance out there looking for scoundrels like ourselves. Let's give this some time to quiet down before we attempt to land you."

Lasadi stands and stretches. "I'm famished," she says. She glances at Amita. "Let's get something on that burn, then we'll meet you two in the kitchen." She's gentle as she helps Amita with her harness, guides her out of the cockpit.

Raj unstraps himself as well. "Nothing like a wild adventure and a meal to bring together new friends." He grins and swivels his chair to hold out his hand; his face is still bloody from their earlier scuffle. "What's your name, kid?"

New friends? Jaantzen's last real friend died the night he escaped the orphanage and met Amita. Since then he hasn't met anyone he trusted enough to use that word for—including her. He's just assumed friends were something you left behind in childhood along with toys and getting shoved around.

Raj is watching him with an expression Jaantzen can't quite put a finger on. The other man seems amused, but there's no hint of a hidden agenda. He senses it from Lasadi, too: she could take you or leave you, but she's not going to bullshit you.

There's something about these two he implicitly wants to trust.

We'll see, he thinks. *We'll see.*

He holds out a hand. "Willem Jaantzen."

"Nice to meet you, Will," Raj says. "Your girl's going to be okay."

"She's not my girl," Jaantzen says. "I'm in her crew."

"Then I'd be looking for new work if I were you. Las and I are always looking to take on good people. You ever consider space piracy?"

Jaantzen laughs, surprised, then shakes his head. "If I never come to space again, it'll be too soon."

Raj claps him on the shoulder. "Suit yourself. Now, I hope you're hungry. I promised you a feast of Arquellian delicacies, and I've got a feeling we'll have a lot to talk about."

Namasté Prime

Grá Linnaea

On the planet New Vara, there's a party city called Yayo, where the law says the streets must dance 24/7.

The man they called Tether slid easily through constricted masses of dancers glutting Nysta Street, his hands floating belt-high to brush knuckles lightly on the people he passed. He wished he had somewhere to go, someone to see. Still, freshly home from offworld business, he basked in the comfort of bone-vibrating music.

The music, micro-bursts of bomb-bass gabber, slipped like daggers through his iso-shield, bombarded out of ever-present wall speakers. Sheets of nano-amplifiers made every building a subwoofer, every window a tweeter.

The pummeling noise slowly helped him unwind. Other planets were disturbingly subdued compared to the crazy visual assault of Vara. His polarized eye lenses adjusted constantly against thousandfold neon colors and epileptic flashes from sidewalk billboards and floating holograms. Every light synchronized into a billion suns going nova, winking out, in, out, in, to the four-four drumbeat of bomb-bass gabber apocalypse.

He didn't have any friends to look up, not anymore, but one hour off ship he already had a job: find and apprehend—specified alive—one Dirvis Ejiri.

Ejiri was a reincarnation manager at the cognitive backup center. The job was beneath Tether's considerable talents, but someone wanted Ejiri found and would pay good lucre for it. Back in the day he would have shopped all his jobs through the community, but he had driven many of his old friends out of the business. He told himself it didn't matter.

He shopped thirty percent of his wet-ware to the scan, leaving enough attention open to, well, drift around in hot human funk and be bored.

He loosened his face into a lazy mask of feigned drugger slack, contrary to the hyper-amphetamine mix stewing in him. He fingered sub-dermal keys on the sides of his thumbs to control micro doses of cyclo-xylamines and altered phenethylamine into his brain stem. Each tap an acrobatic adjustment, maintaining the thin and precarious balance of quantities of psychoactives, amphetamines and psychedelics prodding and burning his brain.

Unlike posers with their blood-surfing nano drug-systems, Tether drug-surfed manually. He took absent pride in squeezing an extra twenty micro-grams, constantly poised on the edge of overdose.

Even though he was the go-to person for physical presence infiltration, these days it was still hard to garner enough lucre to maintain his high-ticket tech and drug systems.

His ankle-length coat twitched fitfully like a cat tail, its woven AI flagging Tether's attention to something amiss. He thought-triggered a weapons sweep when cool mist blurred his vision. His retinas burned and his heads-up display flashed as his defense system failed. The airborne nano-virus caused his defense bots to congeal over his body in a fetid silver lather. Before his fingers even brushed his burner's holster, he had three brain scramblers pressed against his skull.

The guns' owners, two genblurs and a testo-male, formed a tight orbit, almost muting the constant dance assault around them. One of the genblurs pocketed a palm gun, probably what had delivered the virus that had fried Tether's defense system. Pedestrians flowed past the group like water around a stone.

A periphery systems check told him his secondary defenses were also dampened by a suppressant. Some new sys-virus. His wetware was a mess. The def-shield would cost him thousands to repair. At least his drug system still worked. He thumbed calming THC derivative into his bloodstream.

The right-side genblur leaned close to Tether's ear, fizzing past the iso-shield. He/She whispered silkily through pouting lips, "No trouble or we'll wet you right here." His/Her breath hot on Tether's ear. "Billy-Billy wants to see you."

Shit.

Tether'd done a share of work for BB, most of it after ditching the community, but tried to keep his face-to-face time to minimum. Billy-Billy was intense, especially now that he'd found God.

Rumor had it that he had a new thing about purity and cleanliness, following the one path of divine righteousness. It didn't sound like any of the peace and love ideals had gotten through, though.

Tether scraped his incisors against his lower teeth, blew out a hot breath and thumbed Ecstasy into his system. Empathogen fought with testosterone, unwinding his muscles.

Herded through the crowd, he slushed dead nano slime off his jacket, movements slow and deliberate so as not to spook his captors.

Too much downer, he felt slack and dopey. Lacking a meaningful escape strategy, he continued the scan and match for Ejiri, flicking jittery eyes to each face he passed. He bumped his staticy AI to put seventy percent resources onto monitoring his peripheral vision. It was hard enough for him to identify anyone when one-in-five pedestrians ran flashing adverts across their faces. He cleared the buffer of nearly constant low-level false positives.

Ejiri had disappeared a fortnight ago; Tether's guess was he'd flipped from the utter tedium of his managerial job. The reincarnation process was intensely complex, but entirely managed by AIs. He was sure all Ejiri managed was machines and his own boredom. Yet, the stat-sheet had only been posted an hour ago and six hundred had already signed on for the search.

The genblur on his left said, "You was supposed to be hot shit."

Hard to tell genblurs apart. It was the one with the lips. "Jetlag," Tether said.

The testo-male prodded Tether in the ribs. "Shut it."

Tether ventured a smirk. "It's shut."

The genblur smiled. "Name's Pat." *Of course.*

The guards marched him to the black-tech district. The testo-male ducked Tether's head under the arm of a neon goddess-statue. The three guards followed and pushed him through sticky debris to the back of the alleyway. He'd been here many times but played dumb and let them do the work to lead him to the hidden door.

The genblur named Pat stuck his/her hand up a broken pipe. Red laser light played over his/her fingers and a door appeared amongst the dirty brick.

The three guards led Tether down crumbling stairs and parked him in a darkened basement room. He could smell mold and rat, maybe real, maybe just for effect; it was hard to tell with Billy-Billy.

Then he was alone in pitch black, the outside world silenced.

Like anyone in New Ishvara, Tether wasn't used to quiet or darkness. He started to sweat after a few seconds of disturbing quiet. Then panic, irrational and encompassing, flooded through him. A tiny rational section of his brain thought of sub-sonic hysteria-inducing waves. Billy-Billy liked to soften folks before granting audience. Tether's thoughts reduced to lizard brain. Urine trickled down his thigh. He fumbled an excess of Diazepam till he floated back to low level panic. Any more and he'd OD.

A voice formed in his head. Small and itchy as if from Tether's own subconscious. "He's coming," said the voice.

He fingered the thumb dermal again.

"Coming. He's coming."

He pulled in the last bit of calm he had and faked a sigh. "BB, can we cut the floor show?"

Immediately in front of Tether was Billy-Billy, illuminated by spotlight high above Tether's head. BB wore a tailored suit, ash grey. From the way the fabric stiffened with BB's movements, Tether could tell that it was interwoven with kinetic reactive fiber. Anything hit Billy-Billy faster than a pat on the back and the fabric would be hard as diamond.

Nice suit. Expensive. BB had come up in the world.

He was more surprised to see human eyes in Billy-Billy's head, blue and young. The last time he'd had an audience, BB'd been sporting cyber-eyes, expensive ones, too. It was even more pricey to go back to flesh.

Tether blew cool he didn't feel. "Nice eyes."

A chilly organ chord covered the discomfiting silence. BB's eyes weren't the only change. Nine chrome cruci-fixes, three evenly spaced on each wall, circled the room. Each cross was one by three meters and reflected light like a mirror. The workspace was in its usual state of messy distress, the walls lined with antiquated wooden tables piled with outdated tech: touch screens, keyboards, magnetic storage. Tether knew the antiques were real, but Billy-Billy kept his space hermetically clean. The dust and mess were for show; holographic projectors calcu-lated mote paths, painted everything with a coat of virtual particulates. Everything, that is, but the crosses, which gleamed purity.

The old tech itself was just museum theatrics, even the aroma of dust manufactured by neural fakery. Billy-Billy was classically paranoid and kept all his business on his person.

Tether walked two meters behind him, more unsettled by the crosses than the sub-sonic panic waves. For all his light casual manner, BB must have been pretty intent to drag him here. With Tether's defensive systems fried, he couldn't afford to make BB jumpy, especially in his own lab.

Tether kicked a wooden chair to test that it was real, pulled it to the center table. "So, what's the caper? I'm working."

"S'right, working for me."

He took a breath to parse that. "*You're* looking for Ejiri?"

Billy-Billy smiled. "Partially, mostly looking for you."

Tether thumbed THC, just a tap. "You could call."

"Got something coming down. Need you now, fast."

Tether swallowed pride and anger. "We talking about real lucre?"

"More than you can imagine."

Tether let his arms loosen. "I'm listening."

Billy-Billy leaned back on his heels, smiled like Tether had just hooked himself on bait. "Ejiri had some important data he wasn't supposed to. I believe he was appropriated for the systems knowledge in his head. Some new reincarnation folks on the block."

Interesting. The reincarnation industry was locked tighter than the lucre-guild. Someone must have botched big for Ejiri to have downloaded prime secrets. If Billy-Billy wanted Tether to dig up reincarnation industry data, he must be playing a big power grab. Dangerous to take on the reincarnation monopoly, an all or nothing game.

In concept, reincarnation was simple. A vat-grown clone of the client was infused with their personality backup from the grand database. In emergencies, computers scanned what was left of the deceased and traced their neural pathways, the cognitive-immunal system, and redundant cell memory. From this the AI built a complete holographic being, this was run through a series of checks and balances and compared to the backup from central memory before being inserted into a new clone.

Occasionally someone died without a recent backup. For those unlucky souls, the process of comparing their current, damaged, neural makeup with a distant copy, often produced a holographic being who was, at best... unique. Rich folks kept a constant wi-fi updater in their stem, always downloading into their backup.

So did Tether.

He fingered just a dash of clarity stim. "So another con-glom is moving in to take market share?"

Billy-Billy sat back in his chair. "Not exactly. More of an open source thing. Group calls themselves Namasté." Said the word like it meant excrement. "Want you to find them."

Tether'd heard the name, a fancy tag for a bunch of low level hackers.

BB reached into the inside pocket of his suit coat and pulled out a puter, a nicer model with a silver case about the size of his palm. He held it over the tabletop and fingered the inlaid button.

The gelatinous mass of the processor slid to the table, unfolded and inflated until it formed a translucent screen and keyboard. The screen lit as it stiffened.

Tether got up and circled the table. No doubt Billy-Billy purposely oriented it so he'd have to walk around. He caught a glimpse of a blood-soaked heal-pad affixed to the back of BB's neck. *He'd removed his wi-fi?*

Tether sat at the table and pulled the puter closer. The document on the screen looked like gov-conglom internal memo. Level one stuff. Tough ice to crack to get at this.

Hot pixels wove the myth of Namasté. Soul hackers. Kids forced out of the marketplace, with nothing better to do. Hearsay of tech-phreaks stealing backups of celebrity personalities, to keep as virtual slaves.

Tether barely heard BB say, "I can't upload this to you. This document's so hot I can only show it on screen."

He'd never gotten into the soul scene. Online trades of big name DJs or movie reviewers, altered to function as databases, a backlog of every piece of media the original person had been exposed to. Same for particularly inter-esting dreamers. Some companies' whole business was mini-chip computers for junkies to trip on mined dreams.

According to the gov file the name Namasté appeared around the time "tape-ups" came into fashion, the merging of multiple stolen souls. The richest hackers were the ones who could merge copies, primarily to be downloaded into richies who wished to experience multiple things at once. Tether shuddered. There was still great conjecture about what became of a personality after a tape-up.

He sighed for real. "You want me to find a bunch of kids."

Billy-Billy touched the case to the puter. It deflated as the case vacuumed the rubbery processor into itself with a wet slurp. "Be a bit harder than that, I think."

"Then what?"

"I got some middle man type action to offer. Business."

Tether thought about acting coy, like he had better prospects. Truth was, he was intrigued. He shrugged. "Okay, whatever. This pays well, I assume."

"The search for Ejiri is a smoke screen—but I'll take him if you can get him. Find Namasté, get me in, and I'll drown you in lucre."

Actual sums were agreed upon quickly, Tether acting breezily about lucre he'd have to work twenty years to raise.

"OK, boss." He looked at one of the crosses, couldn't help but poke at Billy-Billy. "Before I go, you need a stim-pack or something?"

BB shrugged. "No thanks T-man, I've got God."

After acquiring a new defensive screen—top of the line, on Billy-Billy's credit—Tether took the light-train cross-town to the hacker slums, train buzzing with slamming trance music. Might as well start asking around the Blood

Bar; the best of the made hackers would be hanging there this time of night.

The Blood Bar was outwardly a gargantuan wooden shack, an expensive reproduction of an abandoned warehouse covered in replica twentieth century wooden boards. The local smell of oil and burnt plastics was real enough though. Even the pulsing dance music of the city center was distant.

He'd spent three fourths of his life in this place, building his skills, altering his body, learning from his betters. Now he was the best and didn't need anyone anymore. He laid fingers on the familiar door. Some claimed it was real wood. The door creaked as it opened, its sound quickly lost in blaring reggae from inside. His nostrils burned with the stench of ethanol-infused liquor.

The Blood Bar earned its title from millions of red LED's embedded in Lucite shaped to form pulsing red tables, walls and bar. Dim and dead LEDs created a sullen texture, like veins in a junkie's skin. Hackers and thugs sat amongst floor-embedded tables, their faces black shadows in demonic light.

The music cut like a stale joke and Tether heard the door behind him bolt with an electric click, simultaneous with a snort from the bar. Darvy, bar owner, ex-hacker, thug, inclined against the faded red surface. His PVC dreadlocks flicked like agitated snakes. Every face turned toward Tether. He thumbed a light THC mix into his system, just enough to give him some cool.

"Hey, Darvy." His voice cacophonous in the new silence.

Darvy's dreads slowly rose, as if with static electricity. "Got a question for you, scab. Just one."

Tether stood immobile. A back-step toward the door might touch off a nasty piece of tech.

Darvy rolled his eyes to the ceiling. "Rumor is you working for Billy-Billy."

Hackers and thugs rose from their tables almost as one. Faces lit as they stood. Not happy faces either. Tether's defense system red-lined with warnings. A number of lethals were gearing up. His new system might keep him alive for a few seconds if this mob went at him.

He restrained himself from dumping more Ecstasy into his system. "What the hell? Just doing some contract work." He raised his hands. "When did everybody get political all of a sudden?"

Folks were looking back to Darvy, as if for permission. He said to Tether, "Maybe you should have stayed off planet."

Tether considered and abandoned plausible lies. Something big was damn well going down about Billy-Billy and Namasté. Tether had never mixed with the soul hacker crowd, but remembered umpteen folks had by the time he'd gone off planet.

A trickle of sweat ran down the back of his neck, pooling against his wi-fi nub. "Check. I took the wrong job. Let's make this good." His voice reverberated off the walls.

Whatever business deal Billy-Billy was planning, it had pissed off a lot of hackers. Sides had been drawn. "Darvy. Maybe someone should clue me in about this Namasté thing."

He swore he saw a few people flinch at the name. Stillness. His system registered a few lethal systems standdown. As his fear dampened, Tether felt a vacuum in his heart. These weren't exactly friends, but he'd grown up with some of these folks; these were people who wouldn't have been seen with soul hackers six months ago. His computer triggered on someone sub-vocalizing, "Are the Krishnas secure?"

He shook off his surprise and pressed his—perhaps illusionary—advantage. "I think I just quit my contract job, you want to correct my world view?"

Darvy's snake dreads softly deflated. Maybe he was considering whether, or how best, to kill him. People looked back to Darvy, waiting. Tether sweated it. If this went south, he considered pushing his defense system to meltdown. This crowd looked like they'd slag his wi-fi anyway. If he was going to die, maybe take a few with him and hope the backup center had the sense to reincarnate him.

Darvy's dreads snapped back, pulling his face tight. "Might be good to look into another trip."

Tether wove a chaotic path through tight alleyways, blocking his net transmitters, spiraling away from the Blood Bar. He'd been off planet six months. Six months! Everyone was suddenly crazy.

His local career was dead now. His name and ID tags no doubt spun across a thousand hacker blogs. In whatever crazy hacker war that was building, he was branded Billy-Billy's boy.

He made the genblur blocks later, just as he'd become sure he'd lost the hackers. No big talent, he/she didn't seem to be hiding. *The lips.* Probably Pat. Tether slipped on some casual and sauntered to him/her.

"Sup, Pat?"

He didn't stop though, assumed Pat would pursue. Best to put a few more casual blocks between himself and the bar. *What did Darvy meant about the Krishnas? Why are so many hackers suddenly into Namasté?*

Pat, bouncing to distant music, keeping pace with him, had his/her cool on too. "About time. I was about to go in there and get you." His/Her smile belied knowledge. Or implied threat.

Tether's drug systems warned he was way above safe dosage levels. He'd need to sit in some peaceful darkness soon, before his heart seized from a stress-drug meltdown. "So."

Pat slid a data chip out of his/her pocket. "Billy-Billy scammed some new intel, wants you to follow it."

Pat maneuvered to block Tether and crossed his/her arms, clearly not about to leave until Tether accessed the data. Maybe Tether was Billy-Billy's boy now. His only option now was to finish the job for BB and take his riches off planet. He faded sideways till they were both in a chest-width alley.

He winced as he pulled out his data reader, accidentally tugged on the skin implant, ridiculously close to his overly-sensitive nipple. Whoever had designed the damn things had made the ribbon-cable too short.

He slid in the data chip and ran a battery of diagnostics. Pure data, no executables. A few clever proto-AI's could theoretically slip by his anti-virals. Not much choice with Pat glaring down at him.

The moment he initiated play, his visuals blacked and he drowned in silence. He was in nothing, so deep it could only be virtually generated. Simple text scrolled across his vision: *You are tapped. Block your thoughts. Billy-Billy intends to use you to bring down Namasté. You are very expendable.*

The message blipped out and he felt the data shift into normal play mode. Obviously, the message had been hacked on post-send. The scene resolved into Billy-Billy's workspace, filled the silence with a single eternal chord. Billy-Billy sat in a chair at his bench. His arm draped over his knee as if he were holding court. One of the chrome crosses glittered in the background.

"Drop the Ejiri search. Found his body at the reclamation plant. His backup is apparently missing from the reincarnation center. Find me something *quickly.* God be praised."

The scene froze, waiting for him to leave a message. Should he tell BB about the Krishnas?

Screw him. He'd give BB a report when he felt clearer about his own safety. The scene winked out and he was back in the alley with Pat. He shook digital webs from his head. With his body spiraling toward drug funk, it didn't help much.

Pat locked eyes with him, looked noncommittal. "Message received?"

He paused long enough to give Pat a meaningful look. "Check."

"You leave a message for BB?"

"Nope."

"Gimme the data-chip back."

Tether dug the chip out of the data-reader and handed it over. Pat palmed it and scooted out of the alley. "Be in touch."

Tether leaned against blackened concrete. *Did Pat give me the message?* He certainly didn't trust Billy-Billy, but what would BB gain from screwing him?

If the secret message was correct, then Billy-Billy didn't want to form an alliance with Namasté, he wanted to destroy them. BB had the resources to do it, too. If the soul-hackers had become some sort of movement, Tether didn't want to be around for the fall out.

He shook his head. Either way it didn't matter, as long as he came out okay, and got paid.

First order of business: get somewhere private and relatively safe, away from genblurs.

He lay in a damp cardboard box with a hired homeless standing bodyguard. A Goog-map of local New Ishvara gave three Hare Krishna temples within an hour's light-rail from the Blood Bar. News feed scans eliminated two as old, established and non-techy.

One had good possibilities. A quick hack into low level gov data showed it was suspiciously close to a T5 hub. He slipped back into reality and got up to pay his guard. Answers now, sleep later.

The temple sagged, a newer skin built with little lucre over an old grungy prefab. Plaster columns held minarets above the original crumbling brown plastic.

Tether scoped it for an hour, hidden in a pile of debris in a doorway. Definitely intense amounts of tech and wiring around the building, but it was hard to tell if signals were coming from the temple or the surrounding businesses. The building to one side listed as data storage, the other a micro-filament company. Heat scans revealed thirty live bodies in the temple.

He slouched across the street and tapped the buzzer. It was broken, so he knocked. Moments later a human-shaped heat signature approached the door. The fake wood retreated to show a stocky guy in Hare Krishna robes.

"Yes?"

"I'm thinking about changing faith. Can I get a tour?"

Chipping faux-gold and murals of dead Buddha-looking people filigreed the main hall. They kicked up choking dust as they walked, the dust too fretting to be manufactured theatrics. The Krishna guy droned on about vegan meals and prayer days.

Tether couldn't get a solid fix on anything. There were tech signals all around, maybe originating in the side rooms his guide was dutifully avoiding. They passed through thick faux-wooden doors. Their surroundings dripped with vivid chalk murals, creating an illusion of depth beyond the walls. The mural depicted garish scenes of what he could only imagine were trees and lakes and disturbingly open plains.

Something was very wrong. His system spiked with sub-audio vibration. There were terabytes of data flowing through this room. His systems couldn't snag anything solid but some astronomic signals emanated from here.

The Krishna took a single step to the side and swung a hand toward the back of the room. "Through the archway is the temple. Please feel free to wander."

Two more steps and he was positioned behind Tether. The monk beamed expectantly.

A knee kick brought the Krishna to the floor. Tether amped his defensive systems to lethal.

"Stay down, baldy."

Heat scan showed at least five guys crowded at the thick doors behind, between him and the front exit.

The Krishna held his knee, his eyes wide with pain. "Tether, don't be alarmed."

They knew my name.

The archway was the only exit. He was being herded. Sank in the walls around the arch were metal poles shaped to match the stonework.

Possibly a nerve system. Time was dragging with the coke in his blood. He needed an exit strategy before the guys in the doorway made their move. Either run at the mob of Krishnas or chance a possible lethal system in that archway.

The monk on the floor said, "There must be a misunderstanding."

Tether jerked him up by his robes, thumbed a second dangerous level of stimulant into his muscles and hoisted the guy over his head. The Krishna sailed five meters across the room and through the archway.

The monk hit the ground, slid through. He looked shocked and winded, but none the worse for the wear.

Not a lethal system after all. The guys at the front door hadn't moved yet. Riding the testosterone/coke high, he stalked through the arch, planning to grab the toady and make him point out a back exit.

A half-step through the arch, his world shattered into fractal patterns, smaller and smaller and then nothing.

He was in a field. Golden sunlight pricked his eyes through his eyelids, burned and choked him. He gasped and dug his fingers into dry dirt.

"Tether, it will be all right. Just focus on your breathing."

He started at the voice, opened his eyes. A mistake. The sun bored into his skull and he cried. He flicked his thumb dermals for Ecstacy, THC, anything.

Nothing happened.

A low itch covered his skin, began to burn up behind his eyes.

"Oh God." His own voice sounded like a lost sob.

"Please, just breathe."

He lifted his hands to cover his eyes. In the blinding sunlight he saw his hands flow like gelatin, light glittered through them. "What's happening to me?"

The voice, behind him somewhere, was kind. "You're acclimating to the system." Concern drifted into the voice. "Although the process is not usually so traumatic."

His body felt as if electricity were surging through it. As if his veins were flowing with fire.

"My drug-maintenance system isn't working."

"A blood surfer?" The voice sounded shocked. "They never should have digitized you."

Hands scooped him up as if he weighed nothing. Suddenly he was in cool shade, next to a river running with rainbow liquid. Even in his delirium, he could see it was not water. The man holding him was balding, maybe in his forties. He lowered Tether into the rainbow. Tether's skin burned cold and he screamed.

The man stepped into the not-water and held the back of Tether's head. "I'm not going to lie to you. There's a decent chance you'll discorporate." He spoke slowly and enunciated, as if Tether were a child. "But it's up to you. I want you to concentrate on your body. Remember what it is to be you."

Cold and fire clashed inside Tether. "Where?"

"You're in Namasté. We've digitized your psyche." A hand held the back of Tether's head. "Your consciousness is trying to cope without the drugs."

Tether's whole body quivered, on the edge of shaking apart. "What do I do?"

"You only exist as your identity. If you don't synthesize yourself, you'll fade into the general consciousness."

An idea, like a lighthouse in the fog, formed in his lost mind. "Why can't I just imagine I have my drugs?"

"Theoretically you can create drugs here. You can change your clothes, make yourself drunk, whatever. But that's not you; it's not your core."

"Who are you?"

"My name was Dirvis Ejiri. Just rest for now. I'll be here."

The pervasive quiet tore at him, no sound but water and breeze. Even Billy-Billy's hysteria-inducing waves hadn't caused him so much paralyzing fear. He sobbed. "Please talk to me."

Ejiri stroked the top of Tether's head. "Namasté, isn't it beautiful?" Tether tried to look beyond Ejiri but couldn't focus his eyes.

Ejiri said, "They didn't start it for altruistic reasons. The project was originally born to create an intensely recursive processor, or a giant encyclopedia, or both. No one remembers. It started with them cramming hundreds of personalities together."

Tether's hands felt as if his fingers had melted off. He couldn't lift his arms. Pain floated away, washed down the stream.

"Eventually they realized what their project could be. You could say they caught religion. Soon hackers were stealing thousands of profiles, tapping into backup signals, all to create a single unified mind. Namasté."

He still felt Ejiri's hand on his head, or imagined he did. What did it mean to be touched in a digital world?

"Lacking the processing power of major corporations, they linked multi-processor torrents on the web. Millions of machines across the planet."

The warmth from Ejiri's hand slowly melted down Tether's brow.

"The last step is to infect the wi-fi network in people's wet-ware, to run Namasté in real time in people's brains. Imagine, heaven running in the back of everyone's subconscious."

As Ejiri continued, Tether calmed. He could feel the water that wasn't water. It was warmer, felt good on his skin now. He had skin, he could feel it. He lifted his arm from the wet. It was an arm, his arm, naked. His skin looked young, as when he was a teenager. Then it changed to older than he'd ever been. The skin grew and lost needle scars. Clothes grew over his arm.

He reached up, squeezed Ejiri's hand, then pushed up from the water. "Where are the other people?"

"Oh, here. Some wish to be seen, some don't. This water is people, the dirt, the rocks, the sky, the sun, it's all people's consciousness."

He wasn't sure he had heard correctly. "Why would anyone want to be dirt?"

Ejiri was looking into the blue, blue sky. "Why choose to experience anything?"

Itchy waves of drug-need rolled through him. His clothes had re-formed. He and Ejiri walked across a blazing field of flowers and watched the sun fall behind iron mountains. The ever-present openness and silence still made him want to curl into a ball. The air smelled in turns like perfume or at other times like chemical burn.

Ejiri walked easily in plain clothes. Tether was convinced Ejiri's face was changing from moment to moment but couldn't remember how it had looked previously.

Tether said, "I'm still out there, unaware that my consciousness has been copied in here?"

Ejiri nodded. Looking at this simple, calm man, Tether felt an unfamiliar feeling: empathy.

Tether wanted to reach out and touch the man's shoulder. "Sorry to tell you, your body's dead."

Ejiri's face flickered like a like a bad vid feed. "I know."

They walked a bit more before Ejiri said, "I killed myself." He grimaced and his form wavered. "My corporal form had too much information on Namasté."

Tether squinted toward the reddening sun, no longer as painful on his eyes. A thought occurred. "You hacked yourself?"

Ejiri walked ahead, following a path toward the mountains "We're slowly starting to break the encryption on primary reincarnation systems." He tapped the back of his neck. "The wi-fi that connects people's brains. That's what *I* brought to Namasté."

Tether thought about Billy-Billy's amputated wi-fi hub. A breeze sifted through his clothes and he shivered. "Couldn't we just, uh, teleport around here?"

"Sure. But I like to walk sometimes."

Ejiri tripped over a stone. He stopped, went back, and carefully placed the stone back where he had kicked it from. After raking the sand around it with his fingers, he brushed his hands.

There was something about Ejiri, this place, that made Tether want to sit down watch the sun setting. He'd known Ejiri for just a few hours and he felt safer with him than hackers he'd known his whole life. He stood and breathed till Ejiri broke his meditation. "We're almost there. It's probably time to start the pitch."

Tether tensed, absently tapped at thumb dermals that were no longer there.

Ejiri said, "We need your help to stop Billy-Billy."

Something that had been nagging Tether found voice. "Billy-Billy found God. Namasté doesn't just threaten his financial interests, he thinks it's trying to replace heaven."

"When a dangerous man finds something to believe in, most of us would do well to get out of his way."

Tether thought about his drug systems. Ejiri had said he could recreate them if he wanted to. He scratched at his arm. "Why don't you bring BB in here. Show him how cool it is?"

"We already brought a copy of Billy-Billy into the system. He discorporated."

Around the next bend, the path opened into a flat valley. Past a sandy depression was a cave covered with symbols that Tether couldn't read, like letters from disparate languages randomly thrown together. Somehow he knew the symbols represented him.

Ejiri said, "You're still out there, working for Billy-Billy. The miserable drug-you. With your help, he might just destroy Namasté."

Tether scratched the back of his neck. "You want me to hack his mind?"

Ejiri shook his head. "The human brain is the ultimate encryption. Sure, Namasté can infect wet-ware and run systems in the background," He tapped his head. "But each of us is the only one who can get into our own id."

"You want me to kill my physical body."

"We want you to hack yourself." Ejiri looked at the cave. "Get your old self to stop Billy-Billy. No one else with a wi-fi can get close to him."

Ejiri picked up a pebble, handed it to Tether. Its texture felt rough, like a thousand stories had been microscopically written on its surface. Touching the pebble, Tether felt like he'd just met someone new. He felt warm.

"Billy-Billy's genblur, Pat's been hacked, right?"

"Pat is here, yes." Ejiri smiled sadly again. "Even if you stop Billy-Billy, you probably won't live through the attempt."

Tether thought about hacking his own head. Not a pleasant prospect. Of course, if he didn't hack himself, his digital existence would end with all of Namasté.

A cynical spike pricked his heart. Maybe he could double-cross these Namasté zealots. Find his way back to his systems, his drugs. If he ran BB the right way, he'd drown in lucre. His form rippled and he feared Ejiri would know his thoughts.

Ejiri said that Namasté went on practically forever, said Tether had forever to explore it.

He took a step toward the cave. Old life, or new life? He was going in the data-stream either way.

With each step, he felt a magnetic pull. He could already sense harsh digital information. His hacker mind clicked with recognition, hard cold logic of his old mind. The thoughts felt seductively ugly. More steps and strategies formed, methods of attack, ways to avoid traps, battle plans.

He'd imagined there'd be a sensation like drifting down a tunnel or white light, something. But he was just there, in his own head. But muffled, distant, "he" not "He". He felt jarred by rumbling dance music. He was a hitchhiker, carried like a child in the back of his own brain.

Sticky half-thoughts drifted just out of reach, sometimes colors or context for unspoken words, almost but not quite discernible. He could sense the skin in his body, the drugs coursing through his veins, but removed, symbolic, distant. The drugs called and he urged his physical self to dose another hit.

A sharper feeling brushed him, the metallic taste of computer systems. He set aside the drug need and reached with non-existent fingers for the wet-ware.

What am I doing? Was he here to integrate with his body or to stop himself to save Namasté? He didn't know. Either way, he needed to synchronize somehow.

A physical hand, his hand, rose to scratch his body's nose. The nails had blood clotted around them. What had he done in the temple?

Why did he care?

His body passed through the black-tech district, certainly headed for Billy-Billy's. Whatever he was going to do, he didn't have much time. His body was clearly going to download the location and specs of the Krishna center. With the information, Billy-Billy would have the building destroyed before they could set up the wet-ware network.

Tether's body stuck his hand into the broken pipe and bloody laser light played across it.

He perceived coherent thoughts now, sequential images and text, slippery like an advert. With the thoughts, the drug need pulled at him all the more. His body was contemplating how to bid up BB, score an extra 100K. The wall became a door and his body stepped through.

Billy-Billy stood stiffly in his workspace. The theatrical systems off. Without dust on everything else, the crosses looked less impressive, just polished aluminum alloy shaped by machines. Clearly BB wanted to get to business right away.

He caught more of his body's thoughts, sharp, quick jabs. The door shut behind him and he felt a dampened panic, in sync with his body for a moment. A low hum that he hadn't sensed before rose from the floor and walls. He detected his body's fear levels rise. His body's defense systems clicked into standby.

His body said, "What's with the power grid, BB? We here to do business?"

Tether felt his way to the on-board computer, could just feel the defined edges of wet-ware and defense systems. But if he concentrated too hard, they slipped away, fell through his "fingers." Still, he noticed, before his body did, the many unfriendly systems spinning up.

Two testo-males, sheathed in stealth suits, grabbed his body by the neck and arms. He sensed what could only be a hand-held neural interrupter at his body's brain stem. If he could just control his body's vocal chords, he could talk to Billy-Billy.

And say what?

He was about to grab harder at the wet-ware when he remembered what Ejiri had told him. Integrating with his body and systems couldn't be done by force.

Letting go, surrendering, he melted into the computer. He ran virtual fingers across the rough edges of the tech systems, more real than his body, which felt like a cloud at the edge of his peripheral vision.

Billy-Billy looked away, toward a darkened corner, fingered a set of rhythmic taps on the pads of his fingers. Tether sensed lethal systems locking onto him.

His body finally noticed. "The hell you doing?"

Billy-Billy rotated and smiled. "Thing is, I've discovered a disturbing new wrinkle. Seems you have a ghost in your machine."

The testo-male tightened his grip on Tether's neck. He felt his body try to trigger defense systems, but something blocked his body's access to the wet-ware.

Billy-Billy strolled over. Tapped Tether's forehead. "Hello? You hear me in there?"

BB stepped back. "Just so you don't die not knowing." He snapped his fingers. A spotlight illuminated the dark corner. There lay Pat, or what was left of him/her. The back of his/her head was messily open and his/her wet-ware system lain out on an adjacent table.

Billy-Billy crossed himself. "I thought maybe I could isolate the virus, but, ah well." He raised an eyebrow at Tether. "Maybe I'll have better luck the second time."

Tether wanted to run, to abandon his body and soak in the rainbow stream for a year.

As if Billy-Billy were reading his thoughts, he said, "I've created an electromagnetic field around my lab. Can't chance that rat in your head getting out."

It was true. Whatever path had been available before was gone. He screamed, trapped in his old mind.

Tether's body shook, unable to even access the drug system. His body said, "Slow it down, boss." He could feel his body's thoughts go shifty and jagged. "I got crucial data up here. Maybe you should cryonic me, do a backup comparison. Root out the virus." He felt sweat tickle down his body's arms.

Billy-Billy scratched his head, as if the thought hadn't occurred to him. "Tis true, if I wet you, I'd have to hire a new infiltrator and they'll have time to move their facilities. What the heck. For old times sake." He motioned behind Tether. "Knock him out."

In a moment, one of the testo-males would clock him or taze his head. He'd be extracted and Namasté would be destroyed. His consciousness pulled into a tight diamond of frustration.

His body couldn't access his defense systems, but Tether realized he could. Wanting to panic and claw, he brushed gently at the systems, nudged pieces together.

Painfully slowly to his digital senses, the defense system amped a non-lethal shock across his coat. The testo-males fell in a rattling heap behind him.

His body said, "Whoa, shit. Stand down."

Billy-Billy snapped his fingers. The chromed crosses twisted in unison, revealing a pack of steel tubes. Silent darts glittered through the light and sliced through Tether's body. The pain was distant, and all the more horrible for that.

His body drained and folded and Tether felt, like a splash of cold water, his old consciousness die. The wi-fi in his neck tried to signal the backup center, but stalled at the electromagnetic field.

The on-board computing systems were suddenly clear and solid to Tether. With panic he clawed through them. His first thought, lasting for an eternal microsecond, was to release a full payload from his drug system, drown in hallucinogens and hope for a pleasant trip that lasted forever.

His consciousness just brushed the drug system when he noticed, through sluggish and dying components, the defense system's meltdown sequence, red and jagged, surrounded by safety codes. In the next few microseconds, he could drug himself or he could save Namesté.

Billy-Billy smiled down at him, as if he had just given Tether a beautiful gift.

It took a few long microseconds to brush the locks away. Another to convince himself. He connected two final pieces of code and the HUD red-lined. Micro-nuke batteries overloaded. His defense systems flashed, spiraled to meltdown with exponential speed. Tether thought of Ejiri and Namasté. Part of him smiled. Through the dying synapses in his body's eyes, he saw Billy-Billy raise his hands to the ceiling lights, a look of rapture on his face. Tether felt time shift. His body inflated and popped, sending a furious wave of energy and heat. Tether's dispersed holographic self's last image was Billy-Billy, the room, and everything vaporize in a snow storm of absolute white light.

Tether stood confused at the cave entrance. He had thought he was walking through, but now he stood a few meters back. He even saw footsteps leading in.

The cave was different somehow. Maybe the symbols had changed. Somehow they didn't seem to represent him anymore.

He shook his head, looked back, was almost surprised to see Ejiri still there.

Ejiri wavered. "It's done."

Tether looked back at the cave. "But I never left."

Ejiri walked around Tether and brushed away the footsteps that led into the cave. "We are now digital beings, my friend." He put his hand on Tether's shoulder, squeezed him. Tether felt a painful warmth in his heart.

Ejiri said, "Everything that leaves here is a copy."

Tether turned to the sunset and let the wind push his hair from his eyes.

My Work Will Change The World

A. W. McCollough

My work will change the world but the university destroys me out of fear and ignorance. This is not the kind of research we want here, they say at the graduate school ethics inquiry. I fold my arms and say firmly, This is breakthrough research that will change life and death. I look for help to my advisor but he shakes his head and looks away. He says nothing. His mustache twitches like a galvanic frog leg.

This work is unethical, they said, illegal, but we will not press charges if you leave today. My advisor will not look at me. His mustache quivers again.

This is ridiculous, I protest, the rats are already dead — there are no ethics involved. I do not kill anything, I recycle materials that would be wasted. I just use the dead rats from Dr. Maarsten's bio lab. Maarsten sacrifices twenty rats for a single experiment, smothers them with carbon dioxide in a plastic box, and there is no mention of ethics. Why accuse me of unethical research when I don't kill anything? Maarsten's work will change nothing; it is a waste of space and materials. My work will change the world.

They do not answer. My advisor leaves the room, leaving me alone with ethics board. Sign here, they say, and you are free to go. You will not mention the name of the university. You voluntarily leave the doctoral program. You will no longer come onto university property. And we will not prosecute.

They push a stack of white papers in front of me, blanks for me to sign my name. The paper slides across the desk with the same dry hiss of Maarsten's plastic kill boxes.

I sign. I do not care, I will find another lab space and another source for the materials needed for my work. I will continue. I know it is the right work.

I walk home from the lab with my half-full cardboard box; my prototype implantables, a few special tools of my own design, a bottle of my special solution, and a picture of Cerberus, my childhood dog. He died but my work could have saved him, I think. I just need lab space and assistants and I will prove it.

It is raining and there is a gray squirrel dead under a tree, fur slicks his body like plastic wrap. His neck hangs loosely, broken. Bite marks indicate a dog, perhaps, killed it. There is room in the box for him and he is also a rodent, like Maarsten's rats. No need to waste fresh material. I'll call the squirrel Cerberus.

I put the squirrel material in the box next to the proto-type implantables. My home lab does not have enough space to properly arrange the materials, but it will have to do. There is light, not very bright, and the refrigerator has a shelf I can use to keep the materials. The squirrel fits on the shelf, next to Johnson's grape jelly.

It is good. Tomorrow I will begin work.

Johnson lives in the other room in the house. He is at the business school for Economics. He is only in the masters program, but he pays half the rent. Now he is sitting at the table watching the squirrel. I hold the remote.

Johnson takes a drink. The squirrel laying on the table sits up at my command. Stands. Waves its tail. Johnson stares. This could be big, he says, very big. He takes a drink.

It is my work, it will change the world, I say. The squirrel's name is Cerberus. For my dog.

Johnson says, I'm surprised that it doesn't smell. And that you had a dog. He takes another drink and shudders. It almost looks alive. How do you do that?

That is my special solution, part of the breakthrough. The material is plasticized but still plastic. I laugh, it is my favorite joke.

What's in the solution? asks Johnson.

Do you have degrees in biochemistry and molecular biology? Do you have degrees in electrical engineering and computer science?

No, says Johnson, I don't.

I shrug and say nothing. I use the remote and put Cerberus into autonomous mode to activate its native behaviors and movements. It runs away from Johnson to the edge of the table. It crouches to jump so I increase its agoraphobia.

It runs back to the middle of the table and huddles, shivering.

Autonomous mode is not very interesting. Even after plasticization and implantables too much of the animal's personality and functions remain. Trained rats still remember their learned behaviors, fear responses, paths through the maze. I don't know what Cerberus remembers, maybe the dog that killed him, buried acorns?

Johnson says, What kind of space do you need? The biohacker lab may have enough.

An LED on my remote blinks—the squirrel is running low on fuel. Autonomous mode is the most fuel-inefficient since it supports almost the entire range of natural squirrel behavior as well as my programmed improvements. Cerberus begins the hibernation sequence and turns in a circle, quickly at first, then slowing. The sugar cube finally runs out and Cerberus lays down again. He is in hibernation mode until I refuel him or his sensors detect a nearby food source.

Johnson leans over the table and pokes the squirrel.

Don't touch Cerberus, I say.

Johnson pokes it again and Cerberus twitches, his subroutines assessing threat and foraging potential.

In hibernation self-protective behaviors are auto-enabled, I say, and implantables will scavenge fuel from available resources.

Johnson says, What do you mean? And as I start to tell him he picks up the squirrel.

Cerberus bites Johnson, teeth bury deep in Johnsons thumb, and his throat convulses, drinking.

Johnson screams, his voice is loud and hurts my ears, his whiskey sloshes and spills over the table, the ethanol smells pure and clean under the impurities. I lift my remote out of the reach of the spreading pool and check the fuel level on the readout. 20%. The implantables seek fuel but blood is not an efficient fuel source, so refueling is slow.

Johnson screams again, Get it off me! Kill it!

He has not listened to anything I've said. I do not make new material, that would be unethical. Besides, Cerberus cannot be killed, he is already dead. I did not kill the squirrel so there are no ethical questions involved. He was dead when I picked him up from ground.

Johnson tries to pull Cerberus off his thumb but he fails to break Cerberus' refueling jaw lock. The behavior was simple to program since it was a modification of wild-type nut-cracking behavior.

Johnson strikes Cerberus against the wall and leaves a streak of red from his thumb the color of a dog collar. I become concerned; if the implantables are damaged control may become impossible. There are many modified behaviors that are undesirable in uncontrolled situations.

Then the remote readout pings, indicating fuel levels are in acceptable range so I toggle Cerberus back into hibernation.

His jaws relax and he drops off of Johnson. I catch him before falls to the table and check his implantables. There is no damage.

Johnson curses at me but my mother is dead so what he suggests is impossible. I tell him this and he shakes his head.

You are fucking crazy, Johnson says and pours himself a fourth glass. He dips his finger in his whiskey then wraps it in a paper towel. Johnson takes another drink. But that squirrel has possibilities, he says.

Yes, my work will change the world, I say.

I am pleased that the refueling programming works in the wild but blood is not very efficient. It takes a lot to keep Cerberus fueled and there is no easily available supply. Johnson is unlikely to donate more.

Sugar cubes provide far more energy than your blood, I say, but Cerberus has already consumed the sugar cubes in the bowl. Do you have more?

Johnson shakes his head and hands me a package of colored candies. I take some out of the shiny plastic bag. Their primary colors remind me of pipette tips, color-coded for size, bright red, and blue, and green, and yellow. But the candies are all the same amount of sugar and the color means nothing. This makes me angry and I hesitate to use them. But there is no other sugar.

Sit up, Cerberus, I say, open your mouth. I put in candies until the his cheeks bulge. Make sure Cerberus has candy, I tell Johnson, the implantables need fuel.

Johnson shakes his head. I don't feed squirrels, he says.

You already did, I say.

Whatever, Johnson says, Anyway, there is a biolab startup incubator near the university, I can get you in. No more experiments at home.

★

I can stretch my arms and touch each glass wall of the room at the biohacker lab. All the bigger rooms are taken. I hear Maarsten raised money for a genetics startup and rented the entire third floor. That is unfair. A waste of space. He is not ethical. He kills his rats and doesn't recycle them.

The florescent light flickers but not enough to induce epilepsy so I take off my sunglasses. I take three candies out of my pocket and place them on the yellowed melamine counter. The luminous flux is barely sufficient to discriminate between the colors.

Johnson says, This was the printer room but I talked them into letting you use it. No one prints anything anymore. And it is all they have available.

The narrow room has the proportions of a kill box but scaled for humans. One point five meters by two meters. The glass wall on my left shows the empty corridor, the janitor's closest, the bathroom with the broken door.

I like the close-wrapped protective walls but I need room for a table, for a materials refrigerator, for a display case. Can my necessary supplies fit within this narrow box?

The fluorescent strip flickers, a single dangling panel that fast-blinks like a playing card in a bicycle wheel. This increases the risk of epilepsy and is not optimal.

But I can add a light for close work and there space, if not for my refrigerator, at least for my camping chest filled with dry ice. The cooler is big enough to hold several blocks of dry ice and the body of a medium sized dog.

The lack of counter space constrains my ability to work efficiently; there just isn't enough room to lay out the materials or equipment properly.

There are other's with genius as well, not just Maarsten. I won't allow him to be the only one at this biohacker lab. Besides, the work must continue no matter the circumstances. Brighter light and more room will come in time.

I sign the lease.

An intern in drab blue pushes a box labeled 'incinerator' past the door. I stop her and open the box. It is full of material from the melanoma lab, mostly rats but a few mice and a rabbit.

The rats are ugly, and their tumor-eaten skins useless, but it doesn't matter since their bodies and brains are intact.

And they fit in the chest.

I contact the lab manager and they agree to give me their waste material for recycling.

The original squirrel, Cerberus, is too dysfunctional to use; the brain goes quickly despite the solution. The formula is not yet perfect.But it is easy to move the squirrel skin onto a rat. The process is interesting and saves material.

Johnson is excited. This is the ultimate in recycling, he says. Reduce the waste stream, lower the impact on the environment and reduce biohazards in landfills.

Yes, I say, and the rats can be programmed to seek out and cull the wild rats in the landfills, farms, even in cities. It is very efficient.

This the ultimate in green pest control! Johnson says. The valley will love this, this will change the world!

Yes, I say. It is my work. It is right. It will change the world. But I need more space.

Johnson from the business school, my roommate, has a connection and there is interest in the valley for my implantables. Theme parks or some such. Johnson says the market is huge; theme park animatronics are expensive, but there are plenty of carcasses left from fur and animal shelters. It is easy to re-skin the carcasses with what is needed and my process makes the materials very lifelike.

Revivr!, Inc., he says; the potential markets are endless – rats catching rats for pest control, science exhibits like that one with plasticized human bodies, but animated! Theme park rides, programmable movie animals, reanimation for people who have lost their pets…He smiles and takes a deep drink.

I remember my dog, Cerberus, that died. Yes, this is a good idea. I will do it. I sign the deal sketched on the napkin; Johnson is CEO and will talk to the valley and get money; I will be CTO and work in the lab. A good arrangement. Johnson promises that when the money comes I will have assistants to help me improve my work and new lab space. Programmers, engineers, and taxidermists. Brighter lights and more room for materials. This is exciting.

Johnson and I fly down with Cerberus in a small box. The skin transfer went well but the disorderly stitches are frustrating. Next time I will hire a tailor.

The investors look at the squirrel and frown, the secretary covers her mouth and leaves the room quickly. The VCs look at each other and stand up.

Just five minutes, says Johnson quickly. One, says the one in the hoodie.

I push a button on the remote control. The squirrel sits up, dances, lifts its top-hat.

Fully programmable! says Johnson. He is an idiot.

I explain—Behavioral algorithms leverages existing neural pathways and engrams, thereby providing full ecological compatibility, I say, Additional programming and modified implantable hardware enable fully custom actions. Autonomous mode expresses surviving pre-processing behaviors and memory traces, but programmable mode is more interesting. The core technologies provide access to basal motor programs, and given lab space and assistants, I can develop a massively combinatorial action repertoire suitable for any situation, I say.

The investors look at Johnson. Fully programmable! he says.

The VCs smile and mutter to each other. Hoodie nods, says, We're in.

Johnson signs the paperwork and now I can move from the biohacker space. I can build a real lab and hire assistants.

This is good. My work needs more hands. It is so tiring to always work alone but it must be done. The work will change the world.

At first hiring is difficult. I am tired of explaining to candidates that there are no ethical questions, the materials are already dead. We do not kill anything.

Johnson increases the salary and incentive options until finally I get some assistants. They are not from good schools, their resumes are ungrammatical, but they are willing to learn. And they know others interested in this kind of work. Slowly, the number of my assistants grows. Engineers to help with the implantables, programmers, a taxidermist. It is enough for now.

Johnson gets a contract for a theme park, and with a museum for animated dioramas. He is excited and celebrates with whiskey; my assistants, the taxidermists and engineers, drink. I do not.

My work is not complete, not perfect. Now that I have sources for material and assistants to help with the work, I must improve the implantables. I work late at the lab and my faithful Cerberus sits quietly on my lab bench, watching. His cheeks bulge with rainbow candies. Early work, but good.

There is so much more work to do, and so many kinds of materials! I have already forgotten the university, Maarsten, the biolab.

Now I can truly begin my work, beyond rats and squirrels. I am excited for tomorrow.

The lab is running well but living with Johnson is intolerable. He throws away any material I find on the way home after work. Even fresh material.

Johnson says I work too much, that I should leave work at work and not put roadkill cats in the fridge.

But it is interesting material and I always take it to the lab in the morning. It is exciting to work on species that are difficult to find from the usual suppliers.

So I find a new apartment, away from Johnson, with room for a workshop. It is good, but the noise from the upstairs apartment is annoying and nearly prevents me from working at night. The man shouts, and the wife and children yell sometimes. It is too distracting for me to work.

I go up and give warning. The man is gone, it is just the wife and the children.

I am a doctor researching important experiments, I tell her, it will change the world, your noise hinders the salvation of mankind. The end of death!

The mother is petite, quiet, apologetic, offers tea and a plate of cookies in a small voice. She has dark circles around her eyes and a shallow smile.

I sit in the kitchen and tell her of my work and she listens respectfully. The cookies taste of dark molasses and ginger, with a slightly bitter aftertaste. Candy is still more efficient fuel for implantables, but I like them. I speak more about my work and she shows me a picture of her boys. This is Danny, she says, pointing.

The father comes home then from his job, suit wrinkled, tie hanging loose, his tired face clenches and flushes deep red when he sees me at the table. The mother introduces me and he nods, then goes to the living room, silent. That night there is more noise than ever, the man shouting and stamping, and I resolve to find a new apartment as soon as possible.

Apartment hunting is slow, the market tight, and I after a month have not found a suitable location with space for a lab. Johnson annoys with talk of progress, quarterly board meetings, and what have I done with all the money.

I have made work, of course. He doesn't understand the importance of the work.

But some do. Today the mother, the one from upstairs, comes to me. Midsummer, and hot, I do not like to move outside at this time of year, or even open the door. But she is persistent and knocks until I cannot ignore her any longer. I open the door.

Doctor, please help me, she says, help Danny, he is hurt. Her hands clench and unclench her pale yellow dress.

Why not an ambulance? I ask, but she shakes her head violently and whispers again, please help.

I do not do house calls, I'm not that kind of doctor, but no matter. I can always see what the problem is and phone the hospital if needed. But the phone is not needed, nor an ambulance. The boy is dead, that is clear from the moment

I arrive. He is laying on the couch, the other boy crying silently in the corner.

Danny, she said, and pats his hand. Can you help him?

He is dead, I say, the hospital will take him to the morgue. It is too hot to leave him here.

No, No, No, she says. Can you help him? Your work, you said?

I think, can I? Yes. A new material, interesting. My curiosity is fully roused. I have not worked on primates yet, but I am confidant in my methods. Yes, I say, I think can, but he must come with me for a day or so.

Yes, she says, yes, just help him, please. Her smile moves jerkily like sugar-starved Cerberus.

I request a family photo for reference and then take the boy to my apartment. The company lab would be better, but Johnson might not understand. He does not like work on primates. He would likely object.

The child is beautiful, delicate. So unlike the squirrels, cats, deer or rabbits, yet like them in his own way. I lay him on the table and turn on the lights.

The ligature marks on his throat are clear. The small burned spots on his arms and legs glisten under my bright fluorescents and the reason for the mother's hesitance to call the hospital becomes apparent. The man's hands would fit the bruises but she must be reluctant to lose an efficient resource for her and her remaining child.

I pause my scalpel for a moment, thankful that I have this opportunity to help the mother and the boy, then I continue.

I process the boy more quickly than I estimated and I am done in only a day. The improved solution works well and he is very lifelike after plasticization. The implantables are bulky, however. He will need to wear a scarf and a hat when they take him outside.

I nod, the work is good.

Sit up, I say, and he does, hands relaxed, calm. Smile, I said, and he does. It is not perfect.

Hmmm. I adjust the remote. Smile again, I say.

He does and his smile matches the picture. The work is finished, he is perfect.

I will return him in the morning.

The mother is grateful but I refuse her money. I do it for love of my work, for the art, I say, it will change the world. There is no need for you to pay for that and anyway I have funding for materials from the VCs.

I give her the remote control. It shakes in her hand and the work responds, arms waving. I take the remote back.

The remote is gesture sensitive, I say, waving the boy to sit, lay down, stand in the corner. Hold the remote steady or you will inadvertently trigger behaviors. I show her the commands for waking, sleeping, refueling.

Autonomous mode is boring, I say, but it is best for school. And always make sure he has fuel. Lollipops work well.

I give her a bag of raspberry lollipops and leave her to practice with the remote. It is finally quiet upstairs and I get considerable work done. The application of my work to primates gives me many new ideas and I work on the applications for the company.

Later, I visit them, the family, and take coffee and cake in their kitchen. The woman introduce me as the doctor who helped Danny. Danny smells funny, he says. The father nods and his coffee cup twitches, slops onto his hand. He says nothing. His face is not red any longer, but pale, and his eyes as bruised as the boy's throat. Perhaps he is ill.

The younger child eats little and will not sit or stand next to my work. It is too bad, they make a lovely pair. No matter, the father does not healthy enough to make new material.

I take a photo for my lab notebook. The father, un-smiling, stands with the remote. The mother clutches the younger boy who leans away from Danny. The younger boy hides his face. Smile Danny, says the father, and Danny smiles. I see that Danny is not in autonomous mode.

Keep him inside and cool during the summer months, I tell them, he should last for years. Make sure he always has a lollipop in his mouth.

The implantables need fuel.

Such a lovely pair together, the thought does not leave me. A lovely pair. The work now feels uncompleted, unfinished, imperfect. For a weeks I wait for the father to recover, to provide the needed material, but he does not.

He avoids me in the elevator, taking the stairs despite his worsening condition.

The work is important, it will change the world, but not if it is incomplete. Eventually a solution occurs to me. There are ethical questions are troublesome but I decide that if the dosage is precise no ethics will be violated. The work is eager, pressing, necessary and will change the world.

I prepare some small candies for the right eventuality. For a long time the chance does not come, and my impatience grows, but all comes to those who wait.

Today, I am on the stairs, returning from work, when the younger child leads the older past me. The time has come at last, but then I frown. Danny has no lollipop, and his jaws are already working, head swiveling, seeking refueling opporunities. This is unsafe, his body mass requires much more fuel than a squirrel. He will be unsatsified with only a finger-full of blood.

Boy, I say, Boy.

They stop.

Danny must always have a lollipop, yes? Always. For his condition. The boy ducked his head but said nothing. Why no lollipop? I ask.

Father took it away, the smaller boy whispers, Father said Danny doesn't need candies anymore.

Your father is wrongheaded and will hurt Danny again if he does this. Here are lollipops for each of you. Go on, have one. It will help you relax. I say. I give them the prepared candies.

The boy is reluctant, but Danny takes the candy immediately. His face calms as he sucks at the sugar. It is not good to let the implantables go hungry, I say. The boy tastes his, it is good. Watermelon. My favorite.

Thank you, the boy whispers. They begin climbing the stairs for their apartment. They are almost to the top of the stairs when the boy stumbles and falls down, sliding past me, his face calm.

I check him. His forehead is dented and he is not breathing. I am upset. He should not have fallen and damaged his head, he should have just gone to sleep. But at least the fall solves the ethical questions, accidental material.

Danny stands quietly, of course, his implantables are not affected by sedative.

Danny, carry your brother, I say, and we go back to my workroom. It does not take long, the second time and with fresh materials, the session is short. Afterwards, I put both of them in autonomous mode and they go home.

I will bring the second remote up tomorrow.

Tonight there is too much noise from upstairs to sleep. The father and mother are both yelling. I planned to take the remote up tomorrow, but today I watch the police bring out the bodies of the parents.

The children sit quietly in the back of the car, jaws working, mouths still bloody. They have no lollipops. The father is a fool. Was. I told him to make sure they always have lollipops and he does not.

I worry about the children. The implantables need fuel

and blood is not very efficient.

Candy works best.

I give some lollipops to the officer watching the children. I know the boys, I say, they live upstairs. A terrible thing. Please give them these lollipops. The officer takes them and tells me to go back to my apartment. I see the EMTs whispering, looking at the implantables. The work is early, but still good and I want to explain the importance. But it is too soon, they would not understand.

The detective interviews me later, asks about the candy. It is for their brains, I say, brains need fuel. I am a scientist. He nods, takes notes, leaves.

I am tired, but there is still time to go to the company lab and work. There is much to be done, but now at least I have assistants at the company lab.

I am tired. I can not sleep.

I have just finished a large commission; an entire forest meadow installation, with moles, deer, squirrels, and even a wolf pup. The pup is harder than usual to secure; licenses for endangered species required Johnson's skills to negotiate. But he is so loud, it is hard to think.

I need time to explore my work, to develop the new implantables. But the assistants are too loud as well. I must come to work when all the staff have left.

Johnson wants to talk about the board meeting, so he comes to the lab. It is late, and the lab, with its tables and knives, electronic work benches and computer workstations, is empty. Johnson and I meet. He pours whiskey for himself and offers none to me.

We need more revenue, our runway is too short – you've been spending too much on the lab and hiring all this staff, he says. Why did you hire all these electrical engineers, the software developers, the taxidermists? We have a board meeting in one week, how are we going to justify all this expenditure?

I need the space and assistants, and brighter lights with adjustable arms, I say, that is why you are here. You talk to the board. You bring the money so I can work, I say.

Adoption hasn't been as aggressive as we thought, there is an optics problem, he says.

No, I say, ocular function is nominal.

He laughs, not what that means, he says. Listen, there is a lot of push–back from animal rights folks, publicity is bad. Both the religious nuts and the leftists hate us. The VCs are nervous.

The new implantables, I say, they will like the new implantables. The design is almost ready, I can begin working with bigger animals, maybe even primates. I just need a few more months for development.

There is a bottle of solution in my drawer. I take it out. It is not entirely ethical. But the work is important.

No! he says. No primates! He is so loud. The optics on that are even worse!

Stop saying that, I say, There is nothing wrong with my work. The eyes are fine. What do you mean?

He laughs, again, and has another drink. No, he says, we will have to cut the staff to extend the runway. Maybe move to a smaller place.

No, that can't happen There isn't enough space now and the work is necessary, urgent. I have no choice. I pour him a drink.

Have this, I say, this is, 'The good stuff.'

You've been holding out on me, I see, he says. One more for the road. He takes a long drink then looks at the glass. Not bad, he says.

Its just biochemistry, I say.

He stands, tosses the rest back, stumbles over a long power cord, and pulls a monitor to the floor. The is a loud crash, the monitor screen breaks. I can't see him and the room is silent.

Johnson? I ask. Johnson? No answer. He is finally quiet.

I call my assistants and give them the rest of the week off. I have work to do. The board meeting is in three days and the new implantables must be ready.

Johnson does well at the board meeting. I was able to remove the dent in his skull and he looks very lifelike. He is in autonomous mode with extra failsafes so he will stay on script and not talk out of turn.

The numbers are better than he expected, he says. We have several new contracts and are experiencing rapid adoption among two of our target markets. He sucks his lollipop. The technology that Revivr! has developed will enable penetration into several new verticals including veterinary solutions, urban and suburban feral animal control, and cattle ranching. A billion-dollar market, he says.

The investors are pleased. And your run-rate? The Board asks, these numbers are very good.

Johnson says, The engineers are excited to be working in greenfield technology. They expect below market salary and long hours. Morale is good!

What about the hate mail? they ask.

The intensifying war has created a new distraction for the media feeding frenzy, Johnson says, the liberals and religious nut-jobs have the war to fight over now. The spotlight is off of us. We still get a few hate letters and articles, of course, but it is dying down. And we have a new marketing campaign running so the optics are improving. He laughs quietly and blinks.

I nod. Yes, the optics are improving.

Johnson says, The new technology, especially, may well have applications in the military vertical. These implantables will change the world! We may have to move to new labs and hire more assistants. And get brighter lights.

The board nods. Johnson smiles. The lollipop makes his lips very red. The board smiles, shakes hands, and leaves.

I give Johnson another lollipop. The lab is safe. It was a good meeting. Johnson looks at me and his eyes squint and roll. His hands raise, clench, fall again, and he takes a halting step toward me.

I move behind the desk and take out his remote control. The failsafes need to be reprogrammed. I enable hibernation mode and Johnson sits quietly in his chair with his lollipop while I finish programming.

When I leave I place a large jar of lollipops on the desk next to him. There is enough to last until tomorrow. And then I will see if he will be useful going forward.

Sometimes I must make hard ethical choices, but it is necessary for the work to continue.

I pace my apartment. We will be moving to new lab space next month. Someplace quieter. The new hires are fitting in well. Johnson is at the lab. He has a lollipop for the night. The brain is deteriorating faster than usual, perhaps because of the whiskey, but he will last long enough to sign his shares to me.

The apartment is much quieter now that the family upstairs has left.

There is a knock a the door, then another, louder.

Go away, I'm working, I say, but the knocks continue.

I open the door. The detective is standing there with more officers. He holds out an implantable. Is this yours? He says.

I take it in my hand and turn it over, admiring the thin spikes and trailing wires. It is the one I used for Danny. I worry they may have damaged it when they extracted it but it is intact. My first primate implantable.

It is only a prototype, but it is good work, I say.

He arrests me. The colored lights are too bright and the sirens are loud. I worry about Johnson, he doesn't have enough lollipops for tomorrow. I tell this to the detective, but he says nothing. He won't look at me. Tomorrow will be interesting at the lab, I think, when Johnson finishes his last lollipop.

My trial is short. I watch the jury foreman cry when they show the pictures of the family, the children, Johnson at the lab, and the assistant that disturbed him in hibernation mode. I lean forward, but do not see Cerberus on my desk.

Where is Cerberus? I ask my lawyer. The squirrel on my desk, next to the picture of Danny? She looks at me and shakes her head.

A protestor in the gallery, she looks familiar, holds up pictures of Johnson, of the children, screaming at the jury. My lawyer motions for a mistrial; the jurors should not have seen those photos, she says, but the judge waves her away.

I will speak now and of course I will tell the truth. I explain to them from the seat, The jurors do not have the requisite knowledge to judge my work, how could they judge me? They make their decision only from emotion. There is no ethical question. I never make material! I only use what is available! The mother asked me to help with the children. And Johnson fell, I did nothing but make him useful afterwards. My work will change the world. And where is my Cerberus? I ask them several times, but the judge doesn't answer.

Consecutive life sentences, the judge says, incarcerate at the Greenhill Asylum. I don't know the asylum, but it is apparently close to my old university. Maybe my advisor will visit and bring journals.

I will ask him about my squirrel, Cerberus.

I have not been in solitary more than a month or two; it is not a punishment; they say they cannot put me in with the rest of the inmates for fear of my life.

I am bored but I have an idea. I am disassembling a radio for the components. There no rats in my cell, but the cockroaches may be sufficient for the basics. I had more equipment in my room as a child, just not the knowledge. The early experiments suffered from practice, not basic theory.

But it is not enough, I need materials. Lab space. Assistants.

Today I have a visitor, the guard says.

Interesting, I never have visitors. The metal shutter opens and the visitor stares, impassive, from outside. Dark suited, glasses, he is from the government, he says, an agency whose name comprises three letters. He asks a question. Yes, I can implant recording equipment as well, I say.

The agency needs spies; birds, rats, small dogs, that can go unseen or unremarked in places that no one from our side can go, he says. He makes an offer. Will you make them our eyes and ears?

Will I have lab space and assistants? I ask. Yes, he says.

I accept.

The lab space in the secure facility has enough room for now, but they do not send me assistants. No one will work with me, they say. I do not believe them. There is much work, so much work, work much like at the company; birds, small animals, but with implantables modified to record audio and video.

They ask for more and more, faster and faster. I perfect the plasticization solution so only a drop is sufficient to catalyze the process through the circulatory system. I work on miniaturization and the implantables are much smaller now.

I can implant them quickly now, I've designed a single spike for the neural connection. The implantables are almost unnoticeable, the long needles hold the device close to the skull. If there is time, a bit of extra fur or feathers camouflages the lump as a tumor.

Birds and dogs don't have cheek pouches, so I make small sugar packets that I can insert into their body cavities. These are single use packets, afterwards, my work will have to find their own fuel. But even the herbivores are able to get enough fuel from nearby living animals, if needed, and the carnivores need no additional programming at all. The original neural patterns are more than sufficient, and I like to think the animals will be happy in their hunting.

I know they will; I programmed their implantables.

I have an assistant, finally.

I am making work for the new war; tropical birds, gazelle, a hyena. I ask for a chimpanzee and they bring me one. A small male. It reminds me of Danny and I smile. But the most important thing is it has hands.

I build a larger implantable for the primate skull modeled on my memory of Danny's and Johnson's implants. The programming is complicated and overrides much natural behavior, but now, with an assistant, I can make more work. The chimpanzee can pass me instruments, carry the small materials to the bench, hold them, and adjust their position during procedures.

I will name him Cerberus, the first of many. The Cerberus has hands, so there is no need of the sugar pouch in its stomach. Cerberus can use lollipops.

I enable the failsafes and activate the remote. Cerberus sits up and I give him a lollipop. I watch Cerberus for a while to ensure that the implantable is calibrated for the chimpanzee. Cerberus could be dangerous if the original personality regains control. But Cerberus responds correctly to my test sequences and so I enable the surgical protocols. We begin working on the next set of materials. The government man comes and watches for a while through the window in the steel door as we work together. Cerberus positions the material as I insert the implantables.

It is good to have an assistant again.

I am concerned. There is not enough space here for production. Not enough room to lay out the materials and equipment. The lack of space slows progress. But still, it is good to have much work, and Cerberus assists. The implantables are programmed for basic surgical tasks and that helps tremendously. With Cerberus's help I am able to make the deadline for the war.

But still the work is piling up; stacks of new organic material in the cold room. I need more assistants but they refuse to bring me any more chimpanzees for Cerberus. The agent says it is unethical.

I do not understand, they are already dead!

I need room for the tables, room for the shelves of electronics, space for the tubs of waste solids and liquids.

I have a plan for a project. A program to build the future. It might work, if I can get enough assistants. But there is the ethical question. How to get enough material to make assistants to join Cerberus? It is a mistake to make material from living creatures. It is unethical. It leads to smaller lab space and no assisstants

Perhaps pieces? Assemble new material from trimmings? No, too slow, reassembly is tedious, and besides, the guards would notice and perhaps investigate.

I will think on it. There must be an ethical way forward.

Can you work on cadavers? On people? the agent asks. There is need for men who, being dead cannot die.

Yes, I say, You know I can. I think of Johnson and Danny. But I will need more space. There are additional electronics required for the implantables.

But you can do it? He asks. Yes. I say. They bring me men, new material; some from training accidents, or fever, some fresh from the covert war. The guards stare when the orderlies wheel in my materials. Some few have watched me work, but none have watched twice.

They guards here will not speak to me, they condemn my work, yet the agency appreciates my work as necessary. My operations give back usefulness from waste material, new troops that can be sent where no volunteers can be. Stronger, faster, undying. Not given to emotional outbursts or refusal to follow orders, as some in this last war have done. Just calm obedience in semi-autonomous mode, thick blood proof against punctures from bullets or knives.

Cerberus holds their heads for the implantables. He shakes. He is already several months old and the process is not perfected yet. Material can degrade under the best of conditions, much less constant work.

I will need more assistants, but now there is much material with hands! So it will be easy. I will save some of this new material to make new heads for Cerberus. They do not need all of it for the war.

Surely they will not begrudge me new assistants, for efficiency's sake.

I have a new project. A secret plan. A plan for the future, for new space and more assistants.

There are many unanswered problems. What about the ethical question? I will not make new material. And even with many assistants at launch, how can I implant enough afterward to maintain momentum? Where to get the material? I don't believe the morgues hold enough, and the material that is there will not be of the best – too old or diseased. Easily stopped, even filled with the plasticization formula.

I will begin the project anyway, perhaps the solution will present itself during development. The project presents significant technical challenges; miniaturization, reducing implantation session duration, reduced fuel consumption, etc.

The session duration is concerning. I cannot implant all the new assistants alone, and the process requires training. But perhaps a simplified, streamline implantation protocol hardcoded into the implantables? I requisition strong metals for the implantable needles, the electrodes that insert into the neural tissue. Titanium.

I receive the test needles from the factories. I set them into the driver handle, a weighted maul with an insert to hold the needle. Come here, Cerberus, I say, and they do, each head standing in a line. I lift the maul and swing carefully, evenly, testing each needle for skull penetration, depth; measure each degree of deformation in the needle; the efficiency of electrical conduction. I make my selection and order an initial one hundred thousand.

The project begins.

The agent is here again today and the guard raises the steel shutters. His face is pale, thin, and his hand shakes holding the clipboard.

Will the process work on a living man as well? he asks through the window.

I think for a moment. Is it possible? Living material? I am excited. Yes, this will work, it must. It is the solution to the ethical problem in the project. I do not make material but I will change the world anyway. The material can be living! This is the breakthrough I've searched for! I will have to enhance the failsafes, adjust the motivations, basic instincts, but it can be done!

Yes, of course, I say, not so difficult, easier in some ways. More painful, of course, but the tables are equipped with straps. There has been some resistance to the program from the higher-ups; they worry about the legalities, or public opinion, some such. Is that a problem now?

No. That has been taken care of, he says. So, will you need more space or assistants?

Yes, I say, More space and assistants.

Very well, he says, good, good. Chimpanzees are no good, but we have plenty of cadavers.

Good, I say.

We can give you another cold room on this floor. The orderlies will fetch what you need. Now, we have a target for you, a subject. The orderlies can help if you need assistance with him. He may be violent, the agent says.

No need, I say. I gesture and Cerberus steps forward from where they stand next to the wall. Their many heads turn to look at the agent. He steps back for a moment and then approaches the window again slowly. He is paler than before.

See? I have kept some material from every shipment, and now Cerberus are my assistants. They can strap him to the table easily. No need for the orderlies.

The agent is silent for a moment, admiring Cerberus. Then he nods and quickly shuts the window in the steel door.

I smile. The agent has given me the answer, at last. Living material is the key to the project. I should have thought of that before, with Johnson and the second boy.

No matter now. I have the way forward. I will begin adjusting the formula and modifying the implantables today.

They bring him in, the terrorist. The living man, my new material. I am curious. The dead material responds only to the stimulus provided through the implantables that override the neural patterns. The material remembers, of course, otherwise the dead soldiers would have been useless. And semi-autonomous mode must be enabled, to allow for instincts, but the implantable controls.

But what about this material? Still living? This is new, but I have made adjustements. The implantables will work within a living tissue, will stimulate his thoughts in accordance to the programmed pattern – but will he be as fervent for the government as for his old god?

I am confidant the new implantables modifications will work. I estimate the man may live as much as six months after processing; long enough to return, to find his home, to perform his programmed tasks. I have loaded the implantable with the images of the men he will kill.

In any case, the implantables will not harm him and the plasticization formula will only make him stronger, more resistant.

And even if he is killed or dies, the implantables will ensure he continues to serve the government.

It is a good plan and an exciting new area of research for my work. The government has shown me the way; living material solves the remaining ethics problem for the project.

The steel door opens and the orderlies bring him in, park the gurney, and back away quickly. Cerberus steps forward, heads swinging, looking for tasks; some hold his arms and legs, others unstrap him and pick him up.

He is very loud, and I do not understand his language. But it does not matter.

I will not harm you! I say, Remain calm!

He does not, he screams louder, eyes wide, staring at Cerberus, at me.

Cerberus carries him to the table, twists him into place, holds him down. This will be a long session and with their hands occupied they cannot change their lollipops, so I give them new ones.

Living material! I am excited to begin.

The session with the terrorist goes well. The new implantable is a success with the living material. The screaming stops early in the session, and the twisting, so Cerberus can release his arms and legs and stand by the wall. After the session Cerberus wipes the blood from the terrorist's face.

The man is much calmer now, quiet, he smiles. I show him the pictures of what he is to do in order to prime the programming, and he nods. Good.

I test the recording and transmission. The signal is clear. He will bring back excellent information. He will perform the assigned tasks. They will give him weapons, knives, guns, a series of faces to find and sacrifice.

The new implantables are hidden, just a lump under his scalp and down his spine. I am disappointed that the secret project is not yet far advanced. I would give him my new implantables to use.

I do not place a sugar pouch. His own metabolism will provide sufficient sugar, while he is alive, but I give him a lollypop as a precaution until morning. He is good work, he will perform his tasks.

The steel door opens and the agent comes to take him. Go and follow his instructions, I say, and the work nods and smiles around the lollipop.

I give the agent the remote and show the basic controls. The terrorist stands, smiles, follows the agent to the door.

Be sure to bring back the implantable, I tell the agent. I need the data for the project.

The work goes well, the terrorist finds his home and performs his tasks satisfactorily. Many are dead, and all the targets. Unfortunately, no data is recovered and the implantable is not returned. I am disappointed. Data is needed to improve the implantable design. This hinders the secret project. But the agent says there will be more living material, now that the prototype is working. I will be able to collect data for the project soon.

The agent comes again with a great commission; there was an incident, he says, many died and several of those responsible were captured. I am to operate. They give me new orderlies to care for the prisoners and transport them to my lab.

I nod, excited. This will greatly advance the project.

The agent continues, They will be sent to their homes and villages; greeted, welcomed as heroes for their duty and honor and faith. And then, after all their friends and family lay sleeping, they will rise and perform their tasks.

It is a good plan, and poses significant programming challenges as well as logistical concerns.

I must order more electronics from the factories. But I am happy, this is good for the project. I will order test parts for my new design. It is also good to contribute again to the world, add to knowledge, to the service of my country.

I am always eager to discover new applications for my work.

Cerberus is a such a good assistant. They hold the material well, and can position them as needed. The new instruments and implantables are also much improved, smaller, more delicate, easier to hide. This is well, as there is much work nowadays; the war has escalated. We send many overseas, lollipops in their mouths to keep them calm until they can be delivered home, back to their families.

I ask for bulk candy deliveries and stockpile them in my lab space. Soon I will need more space. This facility may not have enough room, I already occupy three floors. Four, if I also count the holding cells for the living material.

The orderlies fetch me living material when I am ready.

Nonetheless, I am running out of lab space. But project is almost ready and I will have more space then. It is almost time to initiate the roll-out. The new implantables with titanium needles can be placed with a single, sharp, push, so there is no need for a long session. It is almost time to acquire new assistants and expand my lab again. I will start with the orderlies, then the guards.

I am eager for the project to launch.

At last the project is ready. I have perfected my solution and miniaturized my implantables. They lay in neat rows on the table, each egg held in its cradle, needles down. I have served my country, now it is time for my country to serve me. I am ready to be free.

Cerberus stands in lines, mallets clutched in their hands, their mouths work silently around their lollipops, waiting. Soon, the steel door will open and the work, the greatest work, will begin.

The foreign factory sent me my boxes, my parts, with no complaint, and drop-shipped more to many locations around the country. Tomorrow they will bring the next group of material, and my Cerberus will follow my directions.

I will implant the orderlies, the guards, and all the living material in the holding cells. By this time tomorrow the facility will be mine.

And then the project will come to fruition.

I have learned much from my research with the agency. There is no ethical question; my new implantables do not kill, merely transform.

I will have new lab space, enough for me and all my assistants, and the work will continue.

Cerberus will find new assistants outside the walls. The supplies are ready and the implantables are programmed with the locations of the drop boxes and candy stores, the locations of the new holding facilities. As each new head rises they will gather the supplies to recruit more.

Then, when the country is prepared and the material is waiting, I will leave my home. I will continue my work in the laboratory outside.

I am excited. There are important research questions to be answered and the engineering poses significant technical challenges. But I will succeed; I will end death and change the world. I will have finally enough lab space, and I will have many, many assistants, outside, under the bright sun.

The Cosmic Game
1: The Vacation Not Taken

Mark Teppo

When Douglas emerged from his two-hour session of paired masseuse chakra massage, there was a man waiting for him. Douglas, who was still caught up in the lingering tingle of Tiger Lily's psychotherapeutic massage of his fourth chakra, stared beatifically at the man, who was dressed in the signature purple of the Hidden Paradise Resort & Spa.

"Is it lunch time already?" Douglas asked. He was trying to remember what day of the week it was. Thursdays, he knew, were Andalusian and Malay gastro-fusion . . .

"Mr. Smyth—" The purple-suited man stopped and bowed. Douglas frowned at the man's excessive formality. Douglas wasn't one of those naval-gazing tourist types who struggled with cultural mores beyond their own, but, even by his world-weary standards, the staff at the Hidden Paradise Resort & Spa erred toward obsequiousness. Douglas couldn't remember if he had other engagements that afternoon, and when he brushed his fingers against his wrist to check, he realized he wasn't wearing his watch. How had he let that happen . . . ?

"It's about your bill . . . " the purple-suited one started as he raised his head. His hands, which had been clasped in front of him, parted.

It was only decades of training—some of it burned so deep in Douglas's mind that even a high-pass MRI scan wouldn't register any brain activity when it fired—that saved Douglas's life. His left hand flashed out, fingers stiff, and the edge of his hand fractured the purple-suited man's trachea. Douglas's right foot caught the man's kneecap, and drove it in a direction that it was ill-suited to go.

The man in the purple suit, unable to breath and unable to put any weight on his left leg, neither panicked nor fell down. He was a professional, after all, and the diffuse light cast by the recessed ceiling globes in the Jade Mountain Therapy Wing of the Hidden Paradise Resort & Spa did not glint off the ceramic fiber blade that protruded several centimeters between the fingers of his right hand.

The assassin had been trained since childbirth in the arts of killing. He knew no other existence than one spent calculating eighth generation risk assessments, physiological inefficiencies and skeletal deficiencies, and neuro-optimized biomechanics. When he stabbed someone, he did not miss, regardless of his own compromised condition.

And yet, his blade made no contact when his fist darted out, moving more quickly than the wing motion of the red-throated hummingbird. He should have, in fact, stabbed his target twice already. How had he failed?

If he and Douglas had been discussing this altercation in a more genial fashion—over cups of steaming herbal tea, perhaps, or maybe even with frosted glasses of glacially-strained gin at their elbows—he would realized his mistake. But, as they were, instead, locked in a life and death struggle that would be over within a heartbeat, the assassin never had the opportunity to examine the Venn diagram overlap of Einsteinian relativistic theory and prana chakra alignment. Which is to say: a very small area that would be labeled 'action without thought.'

Douglas, in the aforementioned hypothetical conversation between himself and the purple-suited assassin would have sipped delicately from his frost-rimmed martini glass and said, "This is all theoretical, of course. There are physical limits to what the human body is capable of." And the assassin would have pursed his lips as if he was holding back a derogatory comment—a quite culturally insensitive one, at that—and Douglas would have politely ignored it, because, after all, the man wasn't wrong in that thought.

However, what actually happened in the hallway was the assassin's hand got tangled in Douglas's virgin wool robe, and Douglas, in a sinuous movement that would have garnered an eyebrow of admiration from an octogenarian yogi, slipped free of the garment, threw it over the head of his would-be killer, and darted back through the door to the private chamber where he had been been enjoying the hands-on pleasure of Tiger Lily and Lotus Flower.

And it was only then, with his naked back pressed against the oaken door of the massage room, that Douglas D. Douglas—field agent of the Territorial Liaison Agency, the most notorious three-lettered organization in AmericaOne—realized he had been compromised.

Douglas was a professional as well, and he was not the sort who dallied in the wake of a surprise assassination attempt to wonder at the why and what-for. He was the sort who focused on more critical things—like pants, for instance—and while he addresses his current lack thereof, let us take a moment of our own and actually consider the why and what-for.

Now, after the Collapse that even those economists who were taking the weekend correspondence course in the Milton Freidman School of Disaster Economics saw coming, there were a couple weeks of crying, land grabbing, and generally bad behavior on the part of some selfish parties. No one talks about it much—for obvious reasons—and everyone agrees that things got better after UGE was signed. UGE—pronounced with an 'H' by those familiar with the way government policies are actually implemented—became known as the 'All for One and One for All' doctrine, and it paved the way for the military industrialization of North America.

It was at this time that the Protectorate High Command implemented ARSE, brought the STFU online, and unilaterally informed the remaining world governments that they were—in the words of Protector General Hollis G. Washington (no relation)—the WTF's bitches.

Naturally, all military decisions like this come with a built-in economic policy implementation. The gentle caress of the cheek after the open-handed slap, as it were. Since the World Task Force had the Singular Task Force Units—i.e., the giant robots—the rest of the world was informed that they would be responsible for creating threats that the STFU could dominate, thereby providing advertiser-ready content for ChannelOne—the worldwide news network—as well as a "real job for every fucking, slack-footed, inbred, mouth-breather who thinks they have a God-given right to suck at Mamma 'Merica's sweet titties" (in the words of Protector General Hollis G. Washington, of course).

This allowed for the continuing spectacle of giant robots beating the shit out of giant turtles, fire-breathing lizards, freakishly bug-eyed moths, gargantuan apes, and one loathsome squid-faced monster from some "goddamn deep sea aquarium that those fucking pinheaded eco-terrorists at OOSE couldn't have found if they had drained the whole South Atlantic" (cf., Protector General Hollis G. Washington's speech at the AmericaOne Unification ceremony in the spring of 20—).

Anyway, seeing as how Douglas has assured both Tiger Lily and Lotus Flower (the pair of marvelous chakra masseuses who had—let's be honest here—saved his life) that he was, in no way, displeased with their ministrations to his chakras, as well as that persistent knot in his lower back that has been troubling him for several weeks, let us set aside this brief highlight of Protector General Hollis

G. Washington's managerial style, and catch up with our soon-to-be beleaguered super spy, who appears to have left the private massage room by the other door.

Sans pants, apparently.

As much as he liked his watch—that is, to say, Claudia, the built-in operational assistant that was better than a real girl in every way but one—Douglas left it in the massage room. He knew the price a man paid for having a ready answer to every question he might possibly have, as well as satellite-corrected global positioning, realtime stock market updates (in all eight remaining financial exchanges), and four-dimensional meteorological modeling. He hadn't been old enough to have a social media presence during the Orwellian Uprising and the farcical White Hat Wipeout, but he had grown up with his father's collection of vintage pulps, and he knew that with Great Data Accessibility comes Great Personal Privacy Invasion. And so, even though he would miss being able to query the exact chemical make-up of any Big Pharma toxicological agent he would undoubtedly encounter in the next sixteen hours (among other useful things), he knew that TLA's SectionCore had rigorous PISS protocols in place.

It's hard to spook when you've got an always-on network device banging out your location and intent every fifteen microseconds to your agency's Personnel Intelligence Surveillance Service.

Fortunately, in his father's collection of books, there had been a copy of Louis L'Amour's *Last of the Breed*, which was all the outdoors education a young mind needed.

Claudia would have been able to hack the resort's central network and retrieve a wire-frame schematic of the architectural plans of the resort, but Douglas didn't waste any time lamenting lack of TLA Overwatch. Without Claudia, he was blind to the virtual world, but he hadn't survived as long as he had by relying entirely on artificial augmentation. When you were down in the shit, the way you survived was to assume everyone wanted to kill you and that every exfiltration plan came pre-borked.

It's just like the Lotharingia Weekend, he thought, as he padded down the employee hallway connecting the two dozen private massage rooms of the Jade Mountain Therapy Wing.

He and another agency asset had been in Luxembourg City, attending a convention at the Regency Limited, one of Filigree Futures' proof-of-concept smart hotels. Before they could accomplish their mission, anonymous operatives had MollyBloomed the central stack. Every circuit that wasn't instantly fried went all *yes to say yes*, and the entire building went lapdog with a terminal need to please. The hotel had been wired into the municipal infrastructure, of course—IT departments were still in the throes of trying to play nice with others, in those days—and the infected operating system had hived its hedonistic enthusiasm into the utility grid before a hotwire crew managed to burnblacken the whole stack.

Needless to say, Douglas's mission (*just a simple snatch and grab, really*) had been badly compromised. Every smart device within a kilometer of the Regency Limited was compromised, and they were all wide-beaming data to a remote server in some aberrant nation-state that dissolved within forty-eight hours of the exploit at the smart hotel. Douglas got out without being seen, which is saying something in a world where there are more smart devices per square meter than there are human observers. Others weren't as lucky, and there was still unresolved fallout from the mission.

He heard a raised voice behind him. He figured it was either Tiger Lily or Lotus Flower, and he knew his would-be assassin had entered the massage room. For a moment, he regretted what would undoubtedly happen to both of the young women—they were professionals of a different sort, but becoming collateral damage in the clandestine world of inter-agency conflict was not something covered by their insurance policies. Not quite an Act of God, but similar when you got right down to parsing the fine print.

Douglas went through the door on his left. This private massage room was similar to his, though there was a broad-shouldered man with abs that looked like they had been 3D-printed onto his stomach and a blonde woman in the massage table. They were engaged in an activity that Douglas didn't recall seeing on the menu of available services, and the woman's eyes widened when she saw Douglas.

"Oh," she managed between vigorous thrusts of her male companion. "I didn't order a second—"

Douglas, who was naked enough to be mistaken as a backup stud, gestured for her to be silent. He grabbed the woman's robe from the hook on the door. "I was never here," he whispered as he slipped out the front door of the private suite.

It was doubtful the woman heard him, and altogether likely that she had already forgotten his intrusion. The hired help was an impressive distraction, if the way she was hanging on to the edge of the massage table was any indication.

Douglas heard a distant scream, and the sound was picked up and echoed by the walls around him. The light globes in the ceiling went red, and a polite but insistent whoop-whoop started.

The Hidden Paradise Resort & Spa was a haven of tranquility and restoration, after all. It would not reject its guiding principles of inner calm and harmony with something as strident as a fire alarm klaxon. Instead, the hotel made subtler noises, like waterfowl agitated by an seismic undercurrent of magma displacement.

Douglas allowed himself a tiny smile. Someone had tripped the resort's security system, and given the tiny shriek he had heard just before the bird noises started, he suspected the cause of the alarm. Claudia, sensing the proximity of a foreign nervous system, had reacted according to her protocols—which meant that both Douglas's watch and someone's hand were gone. Additionally, the hotel security systems had registered a wide-band distress spike. *Fire! Flood! Act of God!*

That'll do, Douglas thought as he slipped on his stolen robe. Well, *squeezed into* is probably a better way to put it. The bottom of the robe barely covered the top of his thighs, and it didn't reach all the way around his waist. But it covered enough of his lanky frame that he could blend in. Just another startled foreigner whose mantra of perpetual peace had been rudely interrupted by a one-in-a-million anomaly.

Commercial planning committees rarely gave much thought to active spycraft in their facilities, which seems awfully convenient, don't you think? It's almost like some lobby paid them to be blind in this regard . . .

Anyway, Douglas fell in with the other resort attendees who were nervously milling about in the hall. None of them had much practice at fire drills—corporate or otherwise—and they weren't sure which direction they were supposed to go. They flocked like nervous sheep, waiting for a wolf to pop up and pick off the stragglers.

Douglas caught sight of the woman whose "deep tissue" massage he had interrupted. Her hair was wild about her head, and she was wearing one of the lavender smocks used by the staff. Her companion—the one with the impressive ab definition and vigorous enthusiasm—was wearing lavender pants and no shirt. His abs were drawing attention. Oher resort attendees had not used the same air quotes when making their spa reservation as had the freshly fucked blonde woman.

A pair in figures dressed in red created a ripple in the wool-robed sheep, but the duo were not interested in those suffering from mild anxiety and the sort of confusion widely evidenced in the citizenry of developed nations whose basal ganglia have forgotten basic survival instincts. Douglas noted the cases the pair were carrying, and correctly marked them as a medical response team. They were heading for Douglas's room, which probably looked more like an urban crime scene than a spiritual oasis.

He floated through the choppy sea of sad little sheep, angling away from where the red team had gone. His would-be assassin was out of commission, but he had to assume the man was not acting alone. There would be others on-site, and he had to spot them before they saw him.

He had to find a weapon too, as well as some way to conceal it. His clothing situation left very little to the imagination.

While Douglas tries to politely navigate the crowded hall without letting his robe gap in a manner that would make men wonder if he was suffering from dementia and women mark him as an asshole to not get stuck in an elevator with, let's wind back sixteen months to when Protector General Hollis G. Washington gave an ultimatum to the STFU team: Big Boy One, the technological pinnacle of Mama 'Merica's smart boys and girls club, would launch by the end of the year, or the United Global Economy—"HUGE," to those intimately familiar with the way hegemony hides in plain sight—would default, and "all the shit this administration has been pumping into the Northern California Reclamation Basin is going to come boiling back out."

Literally. Protector General Hollis G. Washington was not a man who had any use for metaphor.

And if Northern California got swamped with sewage, that meant key exports of both Napa and Silicon Valley would interrupted. Wine and ideas do not flow well when you've got toxic turds floating in your drinking water.

Some bright bulb on the scientific dream team had pointed out that having the Mark 18—the internal designation for Big Boy One—online didn't mean anything for UGE if the giant robot didn't have a monster to fight. There was a mad dash to clear the room and get out of the Protector General's line of sight after that pronouncement, but when the frenzy settled, it was the TLA who got tasked with finding some sucker—sorry, some nation-state who could be coerced into performing a great civic duty.

Douglas—too clever for his own good—had come up with a plan, and Brazil was chosen to implement that plan. There were "complications" (Brazil's term; as far as Douglas was concerned, things had gone entirely as he had projected), and the monster that had shown up in Panama for the All-American Rumpus hadn't stuck to the script. Fortunately, Big Boy One put a round hole in Squidface's decidedly non-Euclidean mug, and the rebroadcast rights along guaranteed that the lights would stay on in AmericaOne for another year. The illusion of prosperity and global equality that had been promised by UGE was maintained, and everyone went back to work.

Expect the Chinese, who were not part of the Unified Global Economy, and who went off on another round of strident noise about the STFU being just another example of American oppression and imperialism, which was, undoubtedly, going to break the world before it actually brought peace and prosperity to all. Since they had no giant robot of their own, all of this posturing and name-calling was an embarrassing attempt to get ChannelOne coverage. Eventually they disappeared behind the privacy curtain they had coerced Silicon Valley to raise around the mainland. No one knew what was going on in China, and frankly, no one cared.

Well, except for the TLA, who cared a great deal. Maybe too much.

On the commercial side of things, Shangri-la Holdings owned the Hidden Paradise Resort & Spa, though without access to the TLA's fiducial Sniff 'n' Trak algorithm, you'd be hard pressed to navigate the byzantine collection of blind trusts, dead member LLCs, and badly mimeographed third-world registries that were the front-facing business entities of the vertically-integrated conglomerate.

Like many VICs, Shangri-la Holdings operated a sprawling number of hospitality and spirituality sites—forty-seven, at the TLA money hounds' last count—and they were scattered across Tibet, China, Malaysia, Vietnam, and Cambodia.

Shangri-la Holdings knew that *Rustic & Ruined* was in high demand again on Channel One's Getaway Destinations sub-channel. The Hidden Paradise Resort & Spa was built on the site of a mid-twelfth century Buddhist monastery that had been shelled extensively during one of those accidental military incursions that were the hallmark of twentieth-century empire building. The Chinese government, not terribly keen on leaving ruined temples lying around for dissident Buddhists to foment revolution and indoctrinate impressionable young people into a life of pacifistic activism, had been happy to sell the site to Shangri-la Holdings.

Well, not Shangri-la Holdings. The Chinese government had made a deal with Side Porch Investment Trust—which operated out of an unmarked building somewhere in the DFW metroplex—who, in turn, hired Five-Eight International Supplies, Azure Construction Management Ltd, and Celestial Bloom Media Market Consortium. Celestial Bloom assembled a portfolio of bids from a half-dozen architecture firms, most of whom were subsidiaries of SPIT, naturally, and the winning firm hired sub-contractors who had ties to ACM, and so on and so forth, until no one could follow the money.

Anyway, the resulting architectural Wonder of the Occident World jutted out of the side of Karakal—one of the fabled peaks poorly notated on most Western maps—at an approximate elevation of 6, 248 feet, more than a mile up from the valley floor. The main building and the famed Snow Gardens were like those mossy mushrooms that grow from the bark of old redwoods and giant oaks.

A half dozen floors were staggered beneath the sprawling gardens, and the seven towers of the guest suites rose twelve floors above. The Jade Mountain Therapy Wing filled the second of the sub-floors, and it was connected to the Snow Leopard Wellness Clinic by a grand staircase carved into the side of the mountain itself. The staircase continued upward, turning through another full rotation before spilling out into the eastern corner of the North Garden, where there was a sprawling display of rampant statuary—mostly dragons, unicorns, and winged cats.

Having navigated both turns of the grand staircase while we were talking about complicated money laundering practices, Douglas paused at the edge of the sculpture garden. He leaned against a statue of a dumpy unicorn that looked more like a constipated donkey than the stork-like and willowy Beaglian standard—pop culture's indifference to proper attribution when it shoves something into meme space notwithstanding.

The Snow Gardens were open to the elements—the bracing chill of the mountain air being one of the therapeutic benefits of the Hidden Paradise Resort & Spa's remote location—and the ambient temperature was slightly above 20 degrees Celsius. He wasn't chilled, however, because each tile of the Snow Gardens' grounds was individually heated by thermo-conductive coils, and the patented combination of ceramics, industrial plastics, and Icelandic aluminum in each tile distributed heat in such a perfect ratio that guests could walk about the garden completely nude and suffer neither frostbite nor contact burns.

He had swiped a brochure advertising Hystricognathic acupuncture treatments while passing through the Snow Leopard Wellness Clinic, The brochure featured a full-motion vid of the treatment, and he had briefly wished that he had an actual porcupine in hand instead of a high-resolution image loop. Still, the brochure was a bi-fold half-sheet—one of those standard business marketing layouts that optimized the amount of coverage while minimizing the use of paper—and he knew eighteen different ways to refold it into a useful weapon.

He opted for a variant of the Pynchon-Rivauldi Arabesque, which sacrificed length for rigidity, and when he finished folding it, he scraped one of the triangular edges back and forth along the unicorn's horn. The Arabesque was meant for close-up stabby work, much like the unicorn's horn (a categorical description which—like it or not—included the squat carrot-like horn on the Snow Garden statue), but the Pynchon-Rivauldi variant said "get an edge if you can." He wasn't going to do any fancy *mis en place*, but an edge was an edge, right?

Satisfied no one was paying attention, Douglas tucked the folded brochure against the inside of his wrist and gave the sorry-looking donkey—sorry, *unicorn*—a friendly pat on the head before he headed across the garden.

Now, in a situation where a TLA field operative found themselves compromised, the Territorial Liaison Agency's Routines & Techniques of Field Management quite plainly noted that an operative should either exfiltrate from their mission as quickly as possible and destroy any incriminating evidence so as to avoid awkward International incidents. And while it wasn't explicitly stated in the RTFM, "evidence" included the field operative's own person, if that was necessary to maintain agency security. It was an elision in the manual that some found overly dramatic, but Douglas—whose step-father had run the Agency for many years—knew it was more of a budget and morale issue.

The Agency couldn't afford rescue operations, and the threat of compromised security integrity from a captured operative was every accountant's nightmare. *It's best you immolate or explosively decompress*, John had once said to Douglas, back when both were younger and less cynical. *Preferably publicly, so that I can tell the Budget Secretary they don't need to change every password.*

Maintaining a five-nine compliance with the TLA's SLAP—Securitized Localization & Authorization Policy— took a full-time staff of eighteen, by the way. This is the price you pay to make sure no foreign government breaks into AmericaOne's security infrastructure. At least, not by finding someone's password scribbled on a sticky note attached to their monitor.

Anyway, the RTFM said that mission objectives became "get out" or "leave a mangled corpse behind" as soon as an operative believes they have been compromised. There was no discussion about finishing the mission, and yes, while Douglas understood the strategic narrative that lead a brain drain—the intelligence analysis focus group that every department had—to reach such a conclusion, he was not one to simply cut and run because someone tried to shank him after a massage. Frankly, it wasn't the first post-therapeutic spa treatment assault he'd had during his tenure as a TLA field operative, though that time in Barbados had been a case of mistaken identity more than an assault on an AmericaOne clandestine asset, but you never stop and ask too many questions when someone is coming at you with a sharp implement, right?

No, Douglas wasn't going to cut and run until he got answers to *Who?* and *Why?* Besides, he had a mission to finish.

What? Just because it was agency mandated R & R didn't mean it wasn't a working holiday. Douglas was well versed in the classic literature of the field. How many times had James Bond been assaulted while a half-naked woman massaged his kidneys? That's right: often enough that it was basically a spy thriller trope.

A good field operative was never where you expect them, and they were always doing something other than what they appeared to be doing. Other professions called this "magic;" Douglas, having read his L'Amour, called it "basic survival skills." There was a subtle difference, lost on most, which was an oversight that both street-hustlers and deep cover operatives relied on.

Douglas figured there was at least one more enemy agent on-site, maybe a third, acting as overwatch. He glanced up as he approached the ground floor atrium of the Hidden Paradise Resort & Spa. Each of the seven towers of guest suites had twelve floors. There were approximately six to ten rooms per floor, which—Douglas did the math—was more rooms than he could vet in a few seconds. If there was a remote watcher in charge of calling in a drone strike when the ground team failed, he was already dead.

It was best to assume a degree of competency in the other team, and if they hadn't put a high-velocity round through his head already, they probably weren't going to, which was a positive note. But it lead to other questions, like: "Why not?" And "Did they mean to take him alive?" And "Who does abductions anymore?"

The TLA wasn't the only international agency with an Immolation Protocol. In fact, it was only the Swiss and the Icelandic who didn't have such EULAs in place. The Swiss, categorically, didn't sign End User Licensing Agreements with any corporation, entity, or national body. This refusal had made interacting with the rest of the world somewhat complicated, but hey, if they really wanted to stick with the whole neutrality thing, this was a solid way to go about it.

No one was really sure if Iceland had a functional government, much less a covert agency, and getting anyone to answer the phones over there had been an issue for most of the decade.

Privately, Douglas thought governance by petulant adolescents was fairly genius if you wanted an effective isolationist policy, and Iceland had only gotten cold and darker since the Quaternary Syzygy and the Wingate Accords anyway.

Douglas reflected on the purple-suited figure. Slight. Good skin coloration. Facial features that were broadly indicative of Asia, making it impossible to know what sort of cultural stock the man came from (much like Douglas's own "European, but not Scandinavian" skin tone and hair color). What had he said? *It's about your bill . . .*

His English had been impeccable, which is part of what had triggered Douglas's deep-core operative response. *Not British-schooled*, he thought, which is what one would expect with a mainlander, and not even that bland intonation affected by Beltway lobbyists and professional constituent figureheads. There had been the slightest burr of an accent. Something like . . . Krygyzstani? Turkmen?

Douglas wasn't sure. He hadn't kept up on the lexicographical controversy about the Altaic language family.

He missed Claudia for a brief instant. She would have known.

A woman stepped out from behind a shrubbery carved in the liquid likeness of a CGI dragon. She was tall and broad in the shoulders and back, and she was wearing

an amaranth and aubergine colored chupa—the Tibet-
an-style ankle-length robe that was bound at the waist.
Douglas tensed, knowing that the chupa's greatest asset
was the large pocket formed by the sash, and that you
could hide everything from a sawed-off shotgun to an
attack dog in that pocket.

All he had was his brochure, folded in the Pynchon-Rivauldi variant of the Arabesque attack style. It was no
good if she had a weapon that was effective at distances
greater than one meter. He had to get close before he could
use his Arabesque . . .

"I have been wandering the garden for some time," the
woman said, and Douglas keyed in to the exoticism of her
almost-imperceptible accent. "I have been hoping to see
a llama."

Her words caught him off-guard, and it took him a
second to parse what she had said. And what it meant. "I,
I think you are mistaken," he said. "There are no llamas
here. Only lamas."

The woman frowned. Her dark hair was braided, and
her nose was a little too proud and her mouth was a little
too wide. "No? That is too bad. I had been hoping to see
how they contemplate."

"There isn't much to see," Douglas said, finding the rhythm
of her speech. "The pursuit of wisdom is a solitary affair."

"A pity." She frowned again. "What use is wisdom if you
cannot share it with another?"

"It's of no use at all, then," Douglas said. "And that might
be why they contemplate it so assiduously."

Her frown gave way to a broad smile, and Douglas felt like the air had grown thin all of a sudden. "Ah, I have found a llama," she said happily.

"I'm not a—" Douglas shook his head. "It doesn't matter."

She knew the code phrases. She was his mission contact.

"Did you—" She paused, and her gaze went over his shoulder toward the corner of the Snow Garden and the broad staircase that went down into the Jade Mountain Therapy Wing. "Did you kill him?"

Douglas's hand tightened around the Arabesque. "Who?" he asked. In his head, his mission status gauge flipped from "*Tenuous*" to "*Fucked*." She knew the codes, but she also knew about the man who had tried to kill him. How badly was he compromised? His brain ticked over to questions of spatial relations and geometry. *A man, approximately fifty meters from a fence that was two meters high, would have to have a forward velocity of—*

"My brother," the woman said. She shook her head. "I am sorry about him." She lifted her shoulders. "Family. You know how it is."

"No," Douglas said. He was an only child, and his mother, in fact, had raised him herself after his father died. He was away at school before she met someone else, and it was another decade before those two got married. "I don't know how it is."

"He is not my favorite, but he is blood," she said. "I hope you didn't kill him, though you had every right to do so."

Douglas, who was deep in the throes of calculating how long it would take him to reach the fence and vault over it (and part of his brain was overzealously calculating how long the six thousand foot drop would take), decided to cut to the chase. "Are you going to try to kill me too?" he asked.

"No," the woman said. "But I am the reason they want you dead."

"Wait. What?" Douglas asked. "Who?"

He was not doing a very good job of getting those "W" questions answered. The RTFM had some cautionary footnotes about this sort of behavior.

He was spared further confusion with a widening of her eyes, and before she could do anything else, Douglas darted at the woman. He flipped the Arabesque forward, slashing up with it. The woman leaned back like a stalk of grass being lightly blown by the wind. She extended her torso and lifted her chin, and the Arabesque narrowly missed her neck.

She swept her left arm up and over, expertly trapping Douglas's area against her body, and her right hand slipped into the enormous pouch of her chupa. Douglas's momentum brought him up against her, and she reached around his body with her right hand. Douglas heard a tiny noise like a cat farting.

Up close, he realized she was an inch taller than he was, and there were tiny laugh lines next to her eyes and around her mouth.

She hooked a foot around his leg, immobilizing him against her body; he was all too aware of how badly the sash of his stolen robe was knotted.

The weapon in her hand made the funny noise again, and somewhere behind him, a body thrashed against a topiary and then hit the ground.

She frowned, and Douglas used that tiny change in her body position to extricate himself from her embrace. He glanced behind him and spotted a man in a purple suit sprawled on the ground. The dead man's sleeve was tangled in the trailing hoof of the topiary unicorn that had brokered his fall.

"Half-brother," the woman said. "More like a second cousin, actually." Her hand dipped into the pouch of her chupa, hiding the weapon as quickly as it had appeared.

"Well, those always are the shifty ones," Douglas said, feigning nonchalance about bad seeds in the family tree.

"We should go before more show up," the woman said.

"Of course," Douglas said, wondering if she was talking about potential assassins or family members. Or both, actually. "There's no reason for this to get more awkward than it already is," he added.

The woman eyed his robe, and—speaking of awkward moments—Douglas noted he was gaping again.

"You are not dressed for this altitude," she said.

"I'm not dressed for anything," he replied honestly.

She clucked her tongue. "Americans."

"What?"

"I do not understand how you became a superpower."

"I'm not sure we do either. Not anymore, at least."

"But still, your giant robot." She wrinkled her nose. "It makes a giant mess of things."

"I think that's by design," Douglas said. "But how else are we going to fight—"

"Fight? Who is left to fight?"

Doulas attempted to adjust his robe. "It's—it's not important," he said. "We can talk about it later. Shouldn't we be—?"

"Oh. You mean—" And she said a word he didn't understand. He wasn't even sure how her mouth made that sound.

"The what?"

"How do you say it in English? Uh, such a dreary language. Ah, yes. Old One. That's it. The Old Ones. Is that who you are planning on fighting?"

"I'm—I'm not going to be doing the fighting," Douglas said. "Besides, how do you—what makes you think they're coming?"

She favored him with a sad smile. "They're already here."

A steady whup-whup noise filled Douglas's head, and at first, he thought it was his heart. And can you blame him? It's one thing to manipulate Protector General Hollis G. Washington to launch Big Boy One two years ahead of schedule, as well as pull a fast one on the scientific community of an entire South American country so as to demonstrate that Mama 'Merica was ready for chthonic doom walkers from deep space, but it was another thing entirely to be told that the unspeakable and unnameable nightmares that had been pulpishly prophecied a century ago were already here.

And then he realized it wasn't his heart he was hearing, but the quick rotor action of an ancient Sikorsky S-99. The helicopter rose up past the two-meter safety fence that ran along the edge of the rest. It drifted sideways in the crisp air like a giant dragonfly, leaning toward the landing pads near the front of the resort, and then it righted itself, orienting its smoked-glass front toward the North Snow Garden.

The Sikorsky S-99 was technically an advance scout and agile attack helicopter. It didn't have the armament or horsepower of, say, the Sikorsky-Boeing FVL class assault helicopters, but its speed and versatility meant that it could handle the thinner air at altitude.

"Shit," Douglas said.

There was a single minigun mounted on beneath the cockpit of the helicopter. It was more than enough to deal with the woman's cat-farting weapon and Douglas's paper knife.

"Aye-yai," the woman said.

There was something in her voice that drew Douglas's attention away from the helicopter.

"My cousins," she said, a sheepish look on her face.

"Are they *all* trying to kill me?"

She shook her head. "Just my father's side." She clucked her tongue. "It is the larger portion of my family, though . . ."

And speaking of family, there is one final bit of back story we should cover while Douglas and his female companion—who is named Börte, by the way, which is one of the most significant and powerful female names in her extensive family—play duck and cover in the Snow Garden with her two cousins and the Terminal Dynamics GAU-19/AFH minigun that is the standard armament installation on the Sikorsky S-99.

As you may recall, Douglas's mother remarried later in life. She was one of the chief scientists who were WTFed into the WTF, and it was her team who pioneered most of the UI for the STFU. Given the Umbra Ultra Top Secret clearance she carried, it was difficult to have a fulfilling social life inside and beneath the Beltway, but she managed to find someone who had as much security clearance as she did. Even more miraculously, he wasn't an asshole.

John Chanchrey had cut his teeth in an acronym-less spook division that had its origins in a weekly poker game attended by members of the Black Chamber, which was constantly in need of operational funds. When the Black Chamber was formally closed down in 1929, four key cryptographers swore to never be caught in a budget shortfall again, and they formed the ____. It provided key intelligence analysis during the Second World War, and during the Cold War, it was responsible for feeding false intelligence to the Russian bear about the CIA's experiments with LSD, ESP, and [redacted].

After the millennium and the subsequent disregard for governmental and third-estate oversight, deep cover organizations put aside the constant headache of bumbling about in the dark without knowing who was working for whom, and came together under the umbrella of the TLA. John Chanchrey was chosen as Director, Responsible for Assets and Technologies, and one of his first initiatives was building a better communications and intelligence gathering rig for the TLA field operatives,: the Wideband Autonomous Telecommunication & Computational Heuristic device, aka the WATCH.

Since the WATCH had to be smarter than the person wearing it, John needed to talk to some smart people in AI, and through some accident lost to time, he ended up interviewing candidates in the STFU UI division. After taking shit from Douglas's mom about the linguistic differences in the various vowels of the English language, he asked her out for drinks, and, well, let's just fast-forward to the part where John is having a father-son talk with Douglas after the incident with Big Boy One and Squidface.

Well, technically, it's a conversation that never happened since the watches of both men were scrambling all recording devices within a hundred yards. If we asked Douglas about the meeting, he'd qualify it as more of a intelligence debriefing than a "father-son talk," and, to be slightly pedantic, it was a "father-*stepson* talk," but that's just getting away from the important matter at hand.

They were sitting in the breakfast nook of a Georgetown CIA safe house, which is to say a condo that had been forgotten but whose utilities and mortgage were still being paid due to some line item buried on a bill twenty years ago that stapled the financial responsibility of the condo (and a dozen others like it, scattered up and down the eastern seaboard) to some accountant's desk in a bleak sub-division of the Department of Education.

Apropos of the occasion, John had brought coffee and donuts.

Douglas was wearing dark sweat pants and a dark hoodie. He hadn't been sleeping well, and he had brushed off John's comments about his disheveled appearance.

"Your mother's project asked for another ten billion," John said. "Tin Star's reaction was about what you expect."

Tin Star being Protector General Hollis G. Washington, whose penchant for profanity was only eclipsed by his propensity for pennypinching. Not that AmericaOne recognized the copper penny any more . . .

"The program can't be stopped," Douglas said. "The robot has to be ready."

John sighed as he dunked his donut in his shade-grown, hand-picked, and hand-ground bespoke coffee. "Some are asking why," he said. "There's talk on the Hill . . ."

"About what?"

"Maybe it's time we stopped this charade," John said.

Douglas made a face. "That's like the SVR and the CIA deciding to take the weekend off from spying on one another."

John shrugged. "It happened once."

"When?"

"I can't say. Sorry. You're not cleared for that."

"Of course not." Douglas rubbed his face. "So, what? UGE is suspended?" He pronounced the acronym with the implied "H" at the beginning.

"There's talk of building roads for awhile—"

"Why?"

"I don't know, Douglas. Maybe people want to visit the State Parks."

Douglas snorted. "Like the Forest Service would open the gates."

"They might, if they were paid . . ."

Douglas stared at his step-father. "Jesus. They wouldn't . . ."

"The idea's been floated. That's all. It's just an idea."

"Just an idea? Fuck, John. You know how dangerous that is." Douglas ran his tongue along the inside of his lip. "Are you bringing back _____?"

"God, no. What a pain in the ass that was. No, look. We have some brain drains who have been data modeling since BB1. Tracking monetary shifts. Currency indexes. Vegas Book. You know, dark money."

Douglas sat very still. "I see."

"One of their models suggested Brazil's financial default might have been, shall we say, nudged. And once you pull that thread, well, it led to other threads."

"How about that." Douglas reached for a bear claw.

"Yeah, how about that?" John rubbed his chin. "So, on the one hand, we have a South American nation-state that defaulted on all of its international loans. On the other hand, North America's vast financial network could be slaved—with proper authorization, of course—to acquire a broad portfolio of quad-banded sub-prime national derivatives. Now, you get these two hands to shake, and wonder of wonders! North America suddenly owns all of the bad debt in the Southern Hemisphere."

Douglas didn't say anything, nor did John, and the silence stretched between the two men. Finally, John chuckled and reached for another donut. "All for One, and One for All, right?" He broke the donut in half, and offered one portion to Douglas. "No one in AmericaOne cares about how it happened, Douglas. It's done. Everyone is one big happy family. There are always skeletons. There's no reason to go looking for them."

"No reason at all," Douglas said quietly. "But someone did."

John's hand paused near his mouth. "Someone did," he said.

"And?"

"And whoever brokered that deal made a *lot* of money, Douglas." John shook his head. "What if that individual— and I'm not saying it was a single individual—"

"Of course not," Douglas said smoothly.

"But for the sake of argument, I'm going to say 'individual,' okay?"

"Sure," Douglas said. He knew the routine.

"What if this *individual* was an AmericaOne citizen? Did they pay taxes on this . . . what do we call it? This *windfall*. Did they pay taxes on it?"

"Maybe they haven't filed yet," Douglas said. "They got an extension or something."

"Maybe," John replied. "Or maybe they're trying to hide it in an Micronesia data vault or some place like that."

"Seems a bit risky."

"That's what I told them, but Fitzworthy—you remember Fitzworthy, don't you?"

Douglas remained calm on the outside. On the inside, he was less than calm.

He knew Reginald Fitzworthy—or NMR, as he referred to the man, if he even though of him at all. Fitzworthy had been the FAIC in Luxembourg, and Douglas yearned to knock out every one of his teeth. Before he tortured him. But after he questioned him.

There were some outstanding questions he wanted to ask. *Why?* And *What for?* Maybe even *How much?* You know how Douglas gets about questions.

Not surprisingly, NMR had been hard to find since that weekend in Luxembourg, which was further testament of the appropriateness of Douglas's acronymic label.

John ignored the muscle pulsing in Douglas's jaw. "Fitzworthy has the brain drain looking into how someone would divest that kind of cash in order to reduce their tax burden," he said. "They've got a dozen Sniff 'n' Traks farmed out across all those old server farms in Eastern Washington—you know, the ones that browned out the west coast a couple times during the cryptocurrency craze."

The older man finished his donut and dusted the powdered sugar off his hands. "Anyway, officially, I'm supposed to tell you take some R & R. HR mandated. Sorry. You've been in the field too long. You need to use some of that vacation time or they're going to schedule a full psych work-up. Trust me. It's better to take a week off than go through one of those."

He reached into the bag which he had brought donuts and coffee in, and pulled out a hermetically sealed hardback book. "First edition," he said. "You mother says you like those." He put the book on the table and stood up. "Take the vacation, Douglas," he said. "Get some perspective. Work on your bucket list."

He patted Douglas on the shoulder—professional courtesy and not in a fatherly way—and then left the condo.

Douglas stared at the book. It was James Hilton's *Lost Horizon*.

The Terminal Dynamics GAU-19/AFH minigun can fire approximately 2,000 rounds per minute. In the time it's taken us to flashback to the father-son—sorry, *intelligence briefing*—the minigun mounted on the fixed bracket under the front nose of the Sikorsky S-99 fired more than 10,000 rounds at Douglas and Börte. None of these rounds hit either one of them, because that would be bad form, narratively speaking. The North Snow Garden of the Hidden Paradise Resort & Spa, however, had sustained approximately five minutes of full-power property destruction. Which is to say, most of the statuary had been decapitated, the topiaries had been shredded, and many of the garden tiles were now malfunctioning. Plumes of steam cut down on visibility, and the thermal venting had created unpredictable air currents and inversion layers. The carrot-horned donkey in the corner, for instance, was sporting a jaunty cap of finely powdered snow.

Douglas and Börte were closer to the broad patio in front of the resort, but there was thirty yards of exposed terrain separating the war zone that the North Snow Garden had become and the main lobby of the resort, where—five meter tall, thermally-reactive, smart-glass, picture windows notwithstanding—Douglas hoped to find better cover from the noisy helicopter.

"They are Merkit," Börte said apologetically, as if that explained why the cousins have not managed to shred them with a couple thousand 7.62 rounds.

"Meerkats? What?" Douglas couldn't hear her clearly over the noise of the helicopter's rotors and the gnawing noise of the minigun made as it chewed along the edge of the raised bed they were crouching behind.

"Merkit." Börte spoke slowly, enunciating the two syllables more clearly.

"Llamas. Meerkats. I can't figure out what code you are speaking," Douglas complained.

"It's not important," Börte said.

Douglas rolled his eyes and edged up to peek as the tenor of the helicopter's engine changed. It was swinging out past the edge of the resort, turning for another run at them. "Come on," he said, tugging Börte's arm. "We have a chance."

She shook her head and pulled her arm free. "Not in there," she said, nodding toward the resort.

"We can't stay out here," Douglas pointed out. He indicated the mangled statue of a dragon that was missing its head, tail, and wings. All that was left was a stubby body, pockmarked by impacts from the 7.62 rounds. "We're running out of cover."

Börte looked around, and found a large chunk of stone to her liking. "Then we'll have to bring it down," she said. She unwrapped her sash and started folding it back on itself, making it wider.

Douglas ducked back down as the chattering Sikorsky came at them again. The stubby dragon cracked in half under the fusillade of 7.62 rounds from the minigun, and the helicopter roared overhead like a frustrated bear who couldn't seem to figure out how to get its paw into the honey jar.

"What are you doing?" Douglas asked.

"Improvising," Börte said. "What are you doing?"

Douglas looked for the helicopter again. "You're making a sling, aren't you?" He glanced back at her. "They're just going to cut you down when you try to throw that."

She smiled at him. "Not if they're distracted."

"Wait. Me?"

She nodded.

"No, no," Douglas said. "I'm not going to play run rabbit run with them."

Börte wrapped the thick band of her sash around the chunk of rubble, and she let the sling dangle from her hand. "Well, we're not using your sash," she said, nodding toward the front of Douglas's robe, which was gaping even more than it had been fifteen minutes ago.

Douglas, mortified in spite of the imminent arrival of death by minigun, quickly fixed his robe. He cinched the sash tight so that there would be no more wardrobe accidents. "Fine," he said. "I'll be the distraction."

Börte gave him a knowing smile that said she had enjoyed his frantic attempts to cover himself, and Douglas turned away from her to better focus on the important task at hand. He peeked quickly, checking on the location of the helicopter, and then he darted to his left. He popped up on the far side of a row of shredded topiary, and ignoring the shards of shattered rock strewn all over the garden tiles (not to mention those tiles which were no longer able to regulate their temperature coils to the Hidden Paradise Resort & Spa's suggested holistic range of 18 to 24 degrees Celsius), he ran. Like a rabbit.

The Sikorsky whined as its changed direction, and he heard the dreadful noise of the minigun gnashing and chewing through the statuary behind him. He ran faster, not daring to look over his shoulder. He didn't need to know how close the helicopter was. Nor if Börte had managed to make her improvised sling work. All that mattered was running.

Rounds leave the Terminal Dynamics GAU-19/AFH minigun at speeds in excess of 2,800 feet per second, by the way. Douglas wasn't going to outrun anything.

The helicopter made a banging noise, and the relentless sound of the minigun stopped. The engine's pitch changed to a shrill whine, and as Douglas looked over his shoulder, the Sikorsky's nose dipped and the whole helicopter flipped sideways. It flipped too far, and its rotors swiped at a sturdy-looking dragon statue that had not yet lost its rampant ferocity. The dragon statue grabbed at the helicopter, causing it to make an ungainly twitch to the left. It plowed into the garden, and to Douglas's dismay, the rotors snapped off as they smacked into the ground. He dove behind a row of smiling stone cats, and pieces of the helicopter rotors skewered, sectioned, and hacked off parts of the cats.

He heard something explode, and he rolled over to watch the edge of a greasy cloud rise and disperse in the inversion layers over the Snow Garden. He had almost gotten his breath back when Börte's face appeared over a headless cat. "Are you injured?" she asked.

His feet hurt, he had skinned his knees when he had gone for cover, and the backs of his thighs were burning from lying too long on a sizzling garden tile, but he didn't see the point of mentioning any of that. "I'm fine," he croaked.

"We should go," she said, and her face disappeared.

Douglas got to his feet, ignoring a pain in his lower back and the stinging on the back of his thighs. *The damn robe was too short!*

Nearby, the Sikorsky was a twisted wreck. It burned merrily, and Douglas could make out the fire-wreathed shapes of two bodies in the cockpit.

Börte shrugged off her chupa. Underneath she was wearing a grey skin suit with straps. What Douglas had mistaken for broadness in her shoulders and back was a tight pack. As she slipped it off, he noted the webbing under her arms that ran all the way to her wrists.

"You're wearing a wingsuit," he said.

Börte removed a set of tight skull caps and goggles from the pack, along with more straps. "How much do you weigh?" she asked, eyeing him critically.

Douglas flinched for a second, thinking his sash had come undone, and then he realized she was assessing him for a different reason. "One eighty," he said. "One eighty-five," he amended under her critical gaze.

"Americans," she sighed. "What is that in kilograms?"

"Uh, eighty . . . I don't know. Eighty-eight? Eighty-four? Something like that."

She shook her head as she attached the extra straps to her harness. "Let's hope it is more like eighty-four," she said. She gestured that he should come closer.

"What . . . what are you doing?"

She held out one of the helmets and goggles. "We're going to jump," she said. She inclined her head. "And hope that you weigh closer to eighty kilograms than ninety."

Douglas looked toward the edge of the resort. "We're more than a mile up," he said.

She started toward the wall that kept resort guests from taking a terribly long fall. "Almost two kilometers," she said. She stopped and looked back at him. "What? Do you have a quicker way down?"

And Douglas D. Douglas—one-time field operative of the TLA, and a man who had seen and done many terrible things—remembered that he was supposed to be enjoying HR-mandated Recreation and Recuperation. And that wingsuiting from an elevation of almost two kilometers, while strapped to the chest of a super spy who might have an even more complicated family dynamic than his, wearing nothing more than a resort robe that most definitely did not cover his entire ass, definitely qualified as recreational.

"No, ma'am," he said. "I do not know a quicker way down."

Börte smiled and held our her hand. "Come on, then. The world won't save itself."

HERE ENDS PART ONE.

KWAK

Jessie Kwak is a freelance writer and novelist living in Portland, Oregon. She writes sci-fi and fantasy with a liberal dose of explosions, gunfights, and dinner parties. She likes to make her readers laugh. She is the author of supernatural thriller *Shifting Borders* and the *Durga System* series of gangster sci-fi stories.

You can learn more about her at www.jessiekwak.com, or follow her on Twitter (@jkwak) or Instagram (@kwakjessie).

"Rogue" hails from Jessie Kwak's *Durga System* universe, a fast-paced series of gangster sci-fi stories set in a far-future world where humans may have left their home planet to populate the stars, but they haven't managed to leave behind their vices. And that's very good for business.

If you enjoyed what you read, get more of the story by joining Kwak's mailing list and downloading "Starfall" for free:

http://jessiekwak.com/get-starfall

LINNAEA

Grá Linnaea is an author, editor and musician living in Portland, Oregon. He's the former editor of *Shimmer Magazine*. He's won *Writers of the Future* and his story "Messages From Valerie Polichar" was nominated for the Stoker Award. Other of his fiction can be found in *Apex* and *Daily Science Fiction*.

You can learn more about him at gralinnaea.com, or follow him on Twitter or Instagram (@gralinnaea).

McCOLLOUGH

Andrew McCollough writes science fiction, fantasy, and undecipherable scribbles. Mostly the latter. His work tends to describe unfortunate things happening to relatable protagonists and often involve magic or robots. He is the author of *Mermaid's Garden* and other short stories and his work is available at Grievous Angel and Amazon.

You can learn more about him at his website: www.andrewmccollough.com.

"My Work Will Change The World" stumbled from the dark and fantastical mind of A. W. McCollough and more stories are emerging all the time.

If you enjoyed "My Work Will Change The World" and want novel updates and freebie flash fiction, then join Andrew's mailing list by downloading a free copy of "The Mermaid's Garden."

https://dl.bookfunnel.com/fhx4089cpt

TEPPO

Mark Teppo divides his time between Portland and Sumner, and he tends to navigate by local bookstore positioning. He writes historical fiction, fantasy, speculative fiction, and horror, and has published more than a dozen novels. If he's writing a mystery, he's pretending to be Harry Bryant.

He also runs Underland Press, an independent publishing house.

You can learn more about him at www.markteppo.com, or follow him on Twitter or Instagram (@markteppo).

If you enjoyed the first part of *The Cosmic Game*, you should check out "All for One," the giant robot story that started it all. How can you get your hands on it? Well, by signing up for Mark Teppo's mailing list, of course.

https://dl.bookfunnel.com/fh7b40lvy1

Teppo sends out a newsletter once a month or so, which will keep you up-to-date on new releases, info on other projects, as well as chatter about publishing and books.

About the Project

This started as a lark, as all projects do.

This quartet gets together once a month or so, and talks shop. One of those conversations revolved around the idea of how writers can interact with their local communities, and someone mentioned an idea about ephemeral readings.

Think flash mob, but less organized, if you will.

The writers would put together a project that had ties to some local landmark. They would put together a book and then have a reading. Copies of that book would be sold at the reading, and when it was over, that would be it. The book would disappear. The crowd would disperse. All that remained was the memory of the experience.

And a couple dozen hard copies in the hands of people who cared.

It's a bit extreme of an idea, but it's not a bad one.

The idea flew around the room a bit—like larks do—and they came back to it again a few months later, and it still made them laugh.

And so they decided to do it.

It seemed fitting to start this series in a bookstore.

Another discussion followed soon thereafter. "What should the anthology look like? What should we call it?" Ideas were bandied about—most of them were too literary for the sorts of stories these writers tend to write—and finally Jessie Kwak said, "Look, my story is about space pirates and space cocaine. I think we should let people know that is what they are getting into, right?"

Mark Teppo said: "One moment, please." And shortly thereafter, the Slack channel dinged and everyone got their first glimpse of the cover of SPACE COCAINE.

There was much silence on the Slack channel, and then finally someone noted: "Well, it's certainly not literary . . . "

No, it most certainly isn't. It's a collection of stories about gangsters and zombies and consciousness uploading and clandestine spy operations, and it's got a giant fuck-all dragon on the cover.

It's okay to shake your head and laugh at the lunacy of it all. We are.

A nod must go out to Joseph Witt at Belmont Books PDX, who graciously allowed us to descend upon his store for the inaugural reading from this project. Independent bookstores are the magical connectors between free-range authors and their prospective audiences. We couldn't make up stories like this if we didn't have people like Joe curating the shelves out there for readers to find our fiction.

Thank you, sir.

More Cocaine

Naturally, we have to flog the drug metaphor well past its usefulness, so here's one more for you.

The first one was, well, it's wasn't *free* free, but it was mostly—okay, *sorta* free. And we know you probably want more. At least we hope you do, and so to be all helpful and accommodating, we've got a sign-up form at our website.

Yes, there's a website.

http://www.spacecocaine.com

Plug your email address into the appropriate form, and we'll notify you when the next shipment of **SPACE COCAINE** is imminent. That way you can plan your budgets and recreational time accordingly.

You're welcome.